WILD LIVES

BONDING WITH BEARS

NICK ARNOLD

ILLUSTRATED BY JANE COPE

SCHOLASTIC

To Dad – with thanks for my very first bear

With grateful thanks to Larry Aumiller of the McNeil River State Game Sanctuary for his expert comments on the text

Scholastic Children's Books,
Commonwealth House, 1–19 New Oxford Street,
London WC1A 1NU, UK

A division of Scholastic Ltd
London – New York – Toronto – Sydney – Auckland
Mexico City – New Delhi – Hong Kong

Published in the UK by Scholastic Ltd, 2003

ISBN 0 439 97865 3

Printed and bound by Nørhaven Paperback A/S, Denmark

Cover bear image supplied by Getty Images. Background supplied by Ardea.

4 6 8 10 9 7 5 3

CONTENTS

CAN YOU BEAR IT?

If you like camping – and you love brown bears ... Wildwatch wants to hear from you!

This summer we need a teacher to watch a bear cub and keep a diary.

- ❑ *Enjoy bonding with brown bears*
- ❑ *Get the thrill of a lifetime!*
- ❑ *Action and adventure in the great outdoors!*
- ❑ *Excellent pay, plus expenses, and travel to Alaska*
- ❑ *Your diary will be published by Wildwatch!*

DON'T DELAY – APPLY TODAY!

"Bonding" means making friends. And I've always dreamed of making friends with a bear because they're my favourite animal. I've been keen on bears all my life. Well, ever since I found out that teddy bears are based on real animals! I'm Ben Adams, by the way, and I'm a teacher.

Actually I'm so keen on bears that I was even dressed up as a bear on the day I saw the advert! Here's what happened…

Imagine me waiting outside my classroom in a bear costume. I was in a cheerful mood. I'd just arrived at school and got changed and I was all set to give my class the biggest School Fancy Dress Day surprise ever!

I lifted my big furry paw and pushed down the door handle. Then I shoved my huge hairy shoulder against the door and leaped into the classroom with a big, scary, bear roar.

"GRRRRRRRRR!" I shouted as I waved my arms in the air.

Some of the children screamed. But not one of them was wearing fancy dress. My heart sank faster than a rock with a lead weight tied to it. Behind the children sat a line of parents who were trying really hard not to laugh. And with them sat the head teacher with a look on her face that spelled danger.

"Mr Adams," she spluttered, "why are you dressed as a bear?"

"It's Fancy Dress Day," I whimpered.

"That's next week!" she thundered. "Today is Parents in School Day!"

A few of the braver children giggled and soon everyone (except the head teacher) was helpless with laughter. I put my paws over my bear face and shrank from the room with a small groan of despair. Luckily no one could see my real face. It was as scarlet as an over-cooked beetroot. I felt 5 cm tall.

The news of my embarrassing mistake spread around the school faster than a nasty tummy bug. When I walked into the staffroom at break I was greeted with a roar of laughter.

"I hear you've been running about in a bearskin," snorted Mr Henley, looking up from his newspaper.

He began to laugh so heartily that he started to hiccup.

"Running about in your bare skin?" tutted Mrs Dwyer, our elderly and slightly deaf librarian. "I don't approve of teachers not wearing clothes!"

"I said bear as in B-E-A-R!" said Mr Henley, loudly. "Hey, Ben, here's something that might interest you." He pointed to an advert in his paper. "These Wildwatch people want someone to go to Alaska to watch bears, ha ha!"

He meant it as a joke. But as I read the advert I felt as if someone had pressed a secret button in my brain. I began to imagine snowy mountains and big brown bears. It looked like my dream job.

Mr Henley nudged me in the ribs. "Are you going to apply, Ben?" he joked.

I rubbed my chin thoughtfully. "Yes," I said. "I think I might give it a go."

Mr Henley stopped laughing and gave me a funny look. As for me, once I'd said those fateful words I just couldn't get the idea out of my head.

So in the end I sent off the form – and guess what? I got the job! I flew to Alaska and that's where my story *really* begins...

THE BEAR BASICS

June 27

I must be the world's luckiest teacher! Here I am in Alaska, just a short plane trip from McNeil River. Every summer scores of bears gather at the river to catch fish. It's the world's number one place to watch bears!

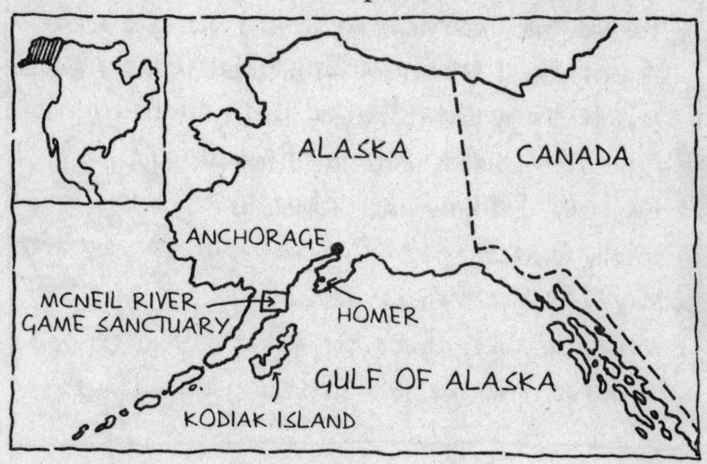

Thousands of people apply to visit McNeil River. But you're only allowed to camp there if your name is pulled from a hat – and even then you can only stay for a few days. I'm going with a bear expert named Jack Douglas, who works as a ranger at the camp, and I've been given permission to stay there with Jack all summer.

Right now I'm staying in a village called Homer, but I'll be flying to McNeil River the day after tomorrow. The first thing I'll be doing is finding a bear cub to write my diary about.

Here's a quick run-down of how I came to be here:

March 15: I dress as a bear. I see the advert and apply for the job.
April 2: My interview for the job. I'm so nervous I'm chewing my fingernails before it starts. But the lady who interviews me is very nice. She seems pleased when I tell her of my interest in bears and says that's just what they're looking for.
April 9: Wildwatch write to offer me the job. Everyone at school is totally amazed.
May 24: My training day at Wildwatch. Mike, that's the guy in charge, gives me lots of bear

Now I'm in my room. My bed looks big and soft and there's even a teddy bear plonked on the pillow! A lot of people think that teddies look like bear cubs – but as you can see, there are a few differences.

And talking about teddies, I can't resist sharing my favourite bear fact with you. Do you know how teddy bears got their name?

BEN'S BEAR NOTES

TEDDY BEARS

1. Teddy bears were named after US President, Theodore Roosevelt. The President's nickname was "Teddy".

2. In 1902 President Roosevelt was hunting black bears, but he couldn't find any. So a captured bear was tied to a tree to give Teddy the fun of shooting it. But Teddy refused to kill the bear. He said it wasn't fair to shoot an animal that had no chance of escape.

3. A New York toy shop started selling "Teddy's bears" and the rest is cuddly history.

Well, I think that's enough for today. My brain is still fired up with excitement, but I'm one of these people who needs lots of sleep. I think I'll tuck myself up with the teddy bear, so night night, everyone!

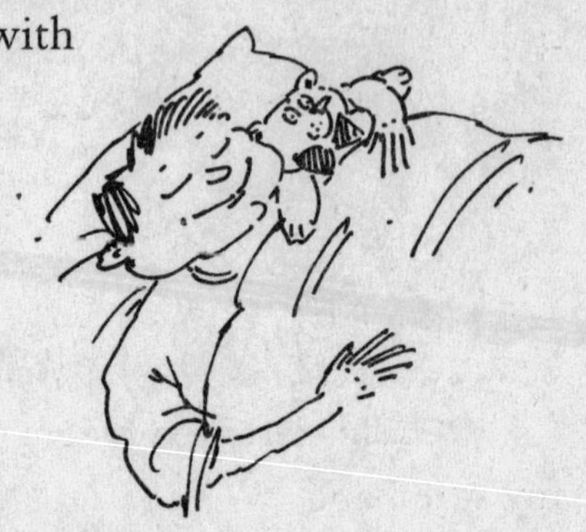

June 28

Today I explored Homer. It's a pretty fishing village named after Homer Pennock, the guy who founded it. The village of Homer faces the beautiful Cook Inlet and has views of snowy mountains all around. The shopping streets are full of art galleries and places to eat and there's a long strip of land sticking into the sea called Homer Spit.

But before I go on, I should tell you about Jack. As I said, Jack picked me up from the motel in Anchorage yesterday. He pulled up in a big, dirty car that spluttered out blue smoke.

"Great to meet you, Ben!" he said with a grin, sticking out a big rough hand and crushing all my finger bones.

"OUCH! Great to meet you, too!" I said, rubbing my sore hand.

Isn't it funny how naturalists often look like the creatures they study? I've seen lion experts on TV with manes of hair and big teeth, and elephant experts with big ears and long noses...

Anyway, Jack, the bear expert, looks a bit like a bear. He's got a bear's big shoulders and a bear's small ears. His beard is grizzled like a bear's shaggy coat. Mind you, Jack's got crinkly blue eyes and bears have orangey-brown eyes.

The drive to Homer took us five hours, so we had plenty of time to get to know each other. Jack's a friendly guy, although he does tend to expect the worst in life. He told me lots of interesting facts about Alaska as we drove along.

I first learned that Alaska is DANGEROUS.

"That's a nice beach," I said, pointing at the seashore.

"It's quicksand," said Jack gloomily. "It's real dangerous stuff. You can sink into it without a trace and the tide rushes in like a wall of water moving faster than you can run. It's a bore."

"It sounds exciting to me!" I joked.

"No," said Jack seriously, "it's called a 'bore' when the tide does that."

Just then we joined a long line of camper vans. The traffic jam was a bore too. Jack huffed crossly and slapped the steering wheel. "City folk!" he exclaimed in a disgusted voice. "Off for the weekend. These mountains are overrun with 'em. At least McNeil River's the true wilderness. There ain't no roads or camper vans or burger trailers where we're headed. Only bears."

Jack knows an awful lot about bears. Well, that's not too surprising – he's been studying bears and watching them in the wild for 20 years. Here are some of the things he told me…

BEN'S BEAR NOTES

THE BEAR BASICS

1. There are eight types of bear in the world: polar bears, pandas, two types of black bear, sun bears, sloth bears, spectacled bears (they're the ones you see in opticians, ha ha) and brown bears.

2. Scientists call the North American brown bear *Ursos arctos horribilis,* which means "horrible northern bear" – sounds scary, huh?
3. "Grizzly" is another name for the North American brown bear. The name "grizzly" may be because the outer hairs of a bear's fur can look grey or grizzled.
4. On average, brown bears measure 1.3 metres (the height to their shoulder) and weigh 362 kg.
5. North American black bears and polar bears also live in Alaska. The polar bears stay in the far north and the black bears mostly live in the forests.

6. A brown bear is usually bigger than a black bear and has a shoulder hump called a "roach".
7. I bet you thought you can tell the bears apart by their colour. You can't! Black bears can be brown and brown bears can be black (and reddish, and blond too!).

8. The biggest brown bears in Alaska live on islands such as Kodiak Island south of McNeil River. These bears, known as "Kodiak bears", can weigh 600 kg – that's equal to EIGHT of me!

I decided to impress Jack with the bear facts I'd learned at the Wildwatch training day.

"Although bears can grow very big," I said, "they're not as dangerous as people think. I've heard that roughly only one person gets killed by a bear in the USA every two years..."

Jack sighed. "You still gotta take care, Ben. Bears are powerful wild creatures with claws as long as your fingers. A bear can break your neck with one paw – and it can eat you too."

I gulped.

"If you respect bears," continued Jack, "and know their ways, they'll put up with you. But if you do something stupid, something that upsets a bear, it can hurt you real bad. Yeah, sure, not many folks get killed by bears but there's always that danger."

We drove past steep snowy mountains and greeny-blue lakes and dark-green pine forests. I saw meadows of tall pink fireweed and purple-blue forget-me-not flowers. We drove through small towns along roads lined with gas stations and drug stores, motels and supermarkets. I'd need a 1,000-page diary to tell you everything I saw!

But that was all yesterday. Tomorrow we're flying to McNeil River, so right now I'm off to bed and maybe I'll dream of having a spit named after me...

June 29

The plane we flew in was something else! If you've ever flown in a plane I bet it was a big plane – something like a jumbo jet. But compared with a jumbo jet this plane looked like a radio-controlled toy!

It was painted red and white and although it had an engine on each wing, there was only enough room for six passengers. Instead of wheels, the plane had floats which looked a bit like jet skis. It was moored in the sea and we made our way along a wooden walkway to reach it.

Hank, the pilot, was waiting to greet us. He jerked our hands up and down, saying, "Mighty pleased to meet you, folks! Now just you relax – we ain't lost a plane yet!"

Once inside, we fastened our safety belts and Hank switched on the engines.

"Let's get this baby into the air!" he called as the plane skimmed over the water like a water skier.

The first few minutes were pure terror. We didn't take off, we sort of bumped into the sky. I'm used to big planes and this little plane's engines just didn't sound right. The aircraft shuddered and juddered and swayed in the wind and I waited in terror for its wings to fall off. Then I looked at Jack. He was sitting back in his seat with his eyes closed and a big smile on his face.

After a while I began to relax too.

I looked down at the waves. The sea seemed to stretch out for ever. Then I spotted a cloudy mountain on an island. Jack said it was the Augustine volcano. Rays of sunshine gleamed through the wispy clouds around the mountain. I couldn't help thinking, "Yikes – that volcano's going to blow at any moment!" I pictured our little plane caught up in the red-hot blast. Luckily Augustine behaved itself.

As we came into land I glimpsed the little bay called McNeil Cove and the river making its way between low green hills. I could see tiny blobs of white where there were waterfalls. I could even make out brown dots. What were they?

"Yep – they're bears," said Jack in a seen-it-all-before voice. "I guess they'll be fishing down there."

"WOW!" I gasped.

In the distance the land wrinkled upwards into grey, rugged mountains. The shape of the mountains reminded me of my knees under the bedspread this morning. But the mountains looked much colder than my knees, with patches of snow on the higher slopes. As we flew lower I got a great view of the camp site and took a photo.

We landed in the cove, just off the beach. The plane's floats sent waves of water whooshing into the air. Then it hit me – I'd have to get out of the plane into the water! I'd brought a pair of waterproof wading boots but they were in my rucksack. I gritted my teeth and gingerly lowered my unprotected legs into the freezing-cold water. The chilly wetness soaked up my trousers like soggy blotting paper.

Waiting on the stony beach were the other rangers, Molly and Brett, together with a few newly arrived visitors. They were all waving. I waved back. People here are really friendly and everyone helps each other. They were all wearing wading boots and they cheerfully splashed into the water and passed our belongings from hand to hand to the shore.

Later, when all our gear had been unloaded, the plane roared into the sky, flying higher and higher, heading towards the snowy mountains before turning to the sea. As the plane's engines faded into the distance, the cove fell breathtakingly silent.

So this was to be my home until September, I thought. It felt incredibly strange to be sitting here. I shivered in my dripping trousers.

"Come on, Ben!" called Jack. "I'll show you around!"

The camp site is a bright-green meadow with muddy paths and coloured tents. Jack showed me the cook shack, the rangers' cabin and the toilet huts in the bushes. I've based this drawing on the photo I took from the plane.

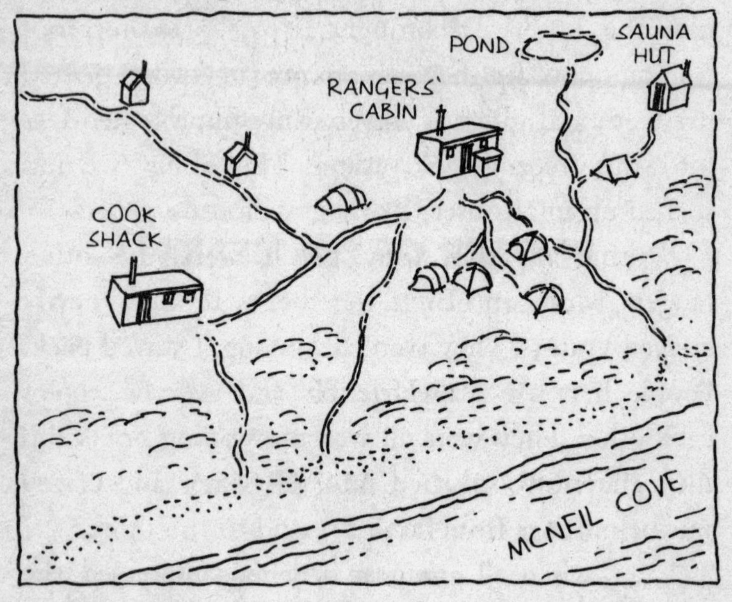

OK, so it's not exactly a five-star hotel but I'm glad to be here.

Tomorrow, we're off to see the bears. I'm pinching myself to make sure it's not a dream. OUCH! No, this is real life! I really am here and tomorrow, for the first time in my life, I'll be seeing real wild bears! Roll on tomorrow – I'm so excited I could explode!

BEWARE OF THE BEARS!

June 30

GOOD MORNING, CAMPERS! It's B-DAY – I mean it's B for Bear Day!

That's what I thought when I woke up this morning. I wriggled out of my sleeping bag feeling chilly but thrilled at the thought of seeing bears.

After breakfast in the cook shack, Jack, myself and eight visitors met up with Molly and Brett.

First came a safety talk from Brett, and I jotted down what he said. You never know when it might come in handy!

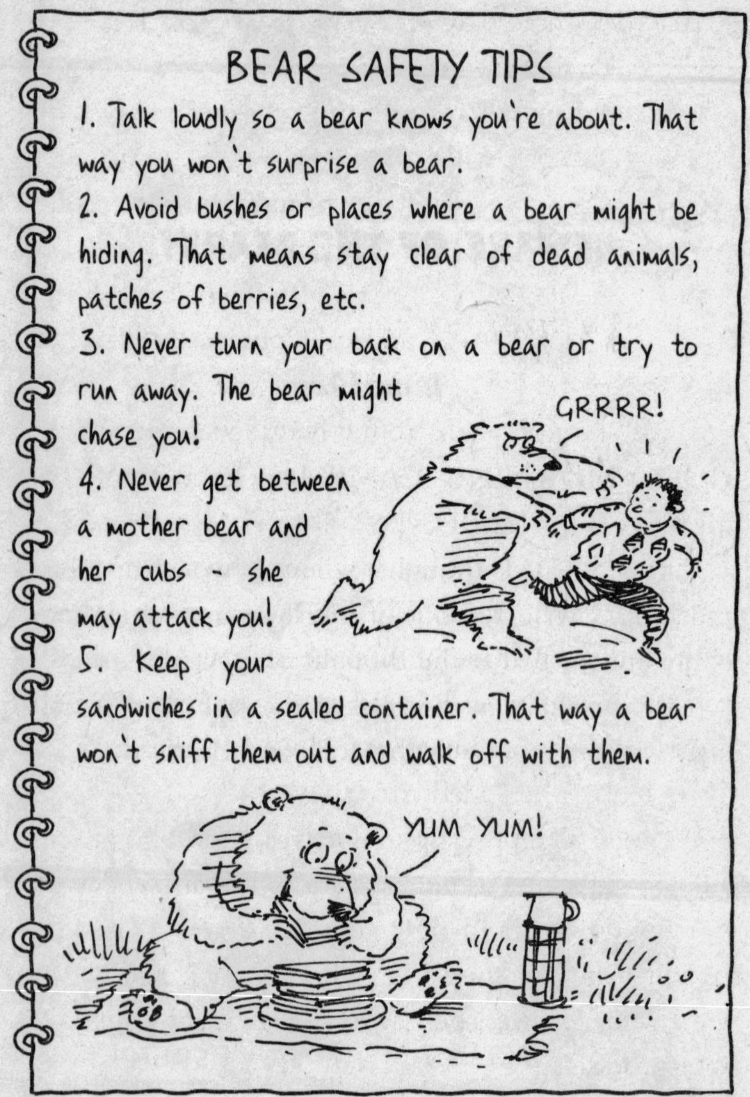

BEAR SAFETY TIPS

1. Talk loudly so a bear knows you're about. That way you won't surprise a bear.
2. Avoid bushes or places where a bear might be hiding. That means stay clear of dead animals, patches of berries, etc.
3. Never turn your back on a bear or try to run away. The bear might chase you!
4. Never get between a mother bear and her cubs - she may attack you!
5. Keep your sandwiches in a sealed container. That way a bear won't sniff them out and walk off with them.

6. Never, ever, walk up to a bear.
7. If a bear comes close, you can climb a tree. Adult bears can't climb. They're too heavy and their claws aren't curved enough to grip the bark.

I pictured myself swinging from a creaky branch with an angry bear leaping up and down and trying to sink its teeth into my bottom.

But Brett grinned and added, "Come to think of it, there ain't too many trees round here. So let's hope the bears are in a good mood!"

We all laughed nervously. It was time to set off.

The morning was misty. There was a pitter-patter of spitty-spotty drops of rain blowing in the wind. Jack said this is what it's like most days round here. "You might get one fine day in a week – and that's if you're lucky!" he added cheerfully.

We were all zipped up in our wet-weather clothes and looked like a gang of giant jelly babies. I was wearing my brand-new blue Gortex raincoat straight from the shop in Anchorage. Jack had on a worn old camouflage jacket over shabby green waterproofs.

We all carried backpacks crammed with everything we needed for the day. Mine held my sandwiches (I wouldn't go anywhere without them!) my camera, this diary and a pencil.

Brett took the lead and we trailed through the long wet grass and wild flowers. Here's a map to show you where we were heading:

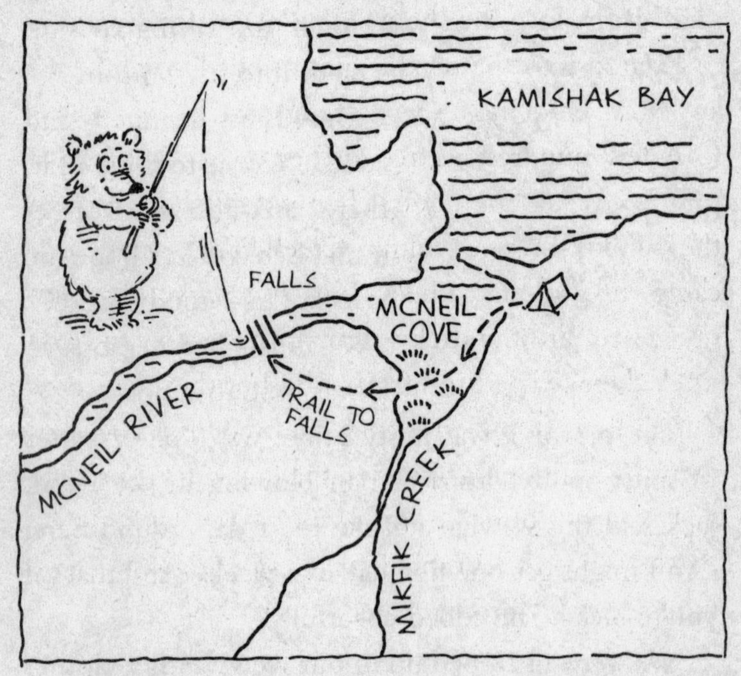

Everyone except the ultra-fit Jack was puffing and panting to keep up with Brett's long strides. I began to feel a bit edgy. I kept wondering what would happen if I got lost in the mist and came across a bear. Would the bear attack me?

Brett led us onto the mud flats and we found ourselves squelching across stones and slimy mud. All I could see was the murky mist and all I could hear was the swish, swish, swish of legs in rainwear and the thwack of the chilly wind against my hood.

At one point Jack stopped me and pointed to a field of grassy plants on the beach. "Sedge plants," he said. "Bears love the shoots, it's a major food plant."

I stared into the drizzly gloom but I couldn't see any bears enjoying a speedy sedge snack.

A few hundred metres further on we stopped to put on our wading boots. Then we splashed through the muddy-brown Mikfik Creek. The water only came up to my knees but suddenly my foot squelched into the sticky-slimy underwater mud and stuck there! I tried to lift my foot but the wader was caught fast so I pulled it from the wader instead. And there I was hopping about in the creek, trying to tug my wader from the mud. But I slipped and tumbled into the icy, muddy brown water.

I staggered to my feet with muddy water spouting from my mouth.

"You OK?" called Jack.

"I'm fine – I really am!" I muttered through gritted teeth.

SQUELCH
SQUELCH!

At last I managed to wrench my wader from the mud. It made a sort of farty sigh – SQUELCH-AHHHH! I tipped a gallon of water from the wader and pulled it on again.

As we made our way onto the dry ground I brought up the rear making sad squelching sounds with every step – SQUELCH, SQUELCH, SQUELCH!

Just then I spotted a footprint in the mud. "Hey what's this?" I cried.

We all gathered round the mark. It looked like a giant human footprint. But why would a giant go for a paddle at this time in the morning? In front of the print were deep slashes in the mud. Claw marks.

"It's a bear's print," said Brett in a matter-of-fact voice.

All the tiny hairs stood up on the back of my neck. One or two of the visitors gasped and everyone started talking at once.

"Looks like the bear wasn't in a hurry," said Jack. "I reckon it was feeding on dead fish that have been washed down the creek."

Of course we all peered around nervously, but there was no sign of the track's maker.

We followed the trail through what felt like kilometres of swishing green grass. Slowly the mist grew thinner and we could make out grey mountains. Then I heard faint sounds. The roar of water on stones. The screech of seagulls. Every time we passed a clump of bushes, Brett shouted, "Hi there, Mr Bear! Good morning!"

"He's warning any bears we're coming," said Jack. "That way they won't be taken by surprise and get mad at us!"

I wondered what Brett would do if a bear popped his head over the bush and wished *him* a polite "Good morning"!

As we trudged on, the roar became louder and louder. At last we climbed up a slope and then ... OH WOW – LOOK AT THAT!

The view was breathtaking!

My eyeballs nearly popped out on stalks!

In front of us was a small valley with a waterfall. About 50 metres of water whooshed and roared over several metres of rocky ledges. Seagulls glided over our heads or stood about on the rocks or bobbed up and down on the bluey-green water.

On its own it was pretty spectacular. But there was more to see. There were bears everywhere I looked – I counted over 20 of them. The first thing that hit me was a sense of the bears' awesome power and strength. I could see their big muscles rippling as they walked. But none of the bears took any notice of us.

Some of them were standing in the river with their noses almost touching the foamy, fast-flowing water. Some of the bears were wandering about on the stony beaches that stretched about ten metres on either side of the river. And there were even a couple of bears sitting in the shallow water like huge hairy men taking a bath. All the visitors had their cameras out and were snapping away like reporters at a Hollywood party. I took a picture too.

As I watched the bears I could see that every one was different. There were big bears, little bears, skinny bears and bears with big bulging bellies. There were smart bears with sleek velvet coats, and scruffy bears with straggly fur that hung down like shaggy old bath-mats. Some of the medium-sized bears had cubs with them and I guessed that they were the mother bears.

A few hours later

Now I'm not one to complain – but one thing was starting to bother me. Well, to be exact there were about 1,000 things bothering me – tiny things with wings. I'm talking about mosquitoes. As the sun came out, the mosquitoes came out too – in force. And guess who had forgotten to put on his anti-mosquito spray this morning?

Jack warned me to use it. "You'd best spray it on a few times," he told me last night. "It'll do some good, but you're going to get bitten, anyway."

Soon the whole mosquito air force was whining around my ears and exploring my nostrils. Every five seconds I had to stop and wave my arms and slap my neck and clap my hands. By lunchtime I was sure they'd already sucked half my life-blood. Why didn't they go for anyone else? They didn't seem to be interested in Jack!

But I'm here to tell you about bears not bugs. I looked at the bear cubs by the river, trying to choose a cub to write this diary about. The trouble was, they all looked the same. What I needed was a cub who looked different from the others. A cub who would be easy to spot. It's hard enough watching bears as it is!

The main viewing place is only a patch of gravel at the top of the high bank overlooking the river. There are no seats and no shelter and definitely no cosy café selling buns and hot chocolate. So I spent the day sitting or standing on the hard stony ground. The longer I sat on the ground the harder it felt. At this rate I'll be going home at the end of the summer with a lumpy, bumpy bottom.

If I want to get a good view of the action, it's best to stand up. And there's always plenty to see! There's another viewing place under some over-hanging rocks beside the stony beach, and from there you can get a really close-up view of the bears catching fish.

BEN'S BEAR NOTES

WATCHING BEARS

1. The great thing about McNeil River is that the bears are used to people. But we humans have to stay at the two viewing places so that the bears won't be too bothered by us.

2. The big male bears like to fish on the opposite bank to the viewing places. The female bears with cubs mostly stay on our side of the river.

3. Maybe the females are scared the males will attack their cubs. Jack says that male bears can attack lost cubs, but it's very rare and he's never seen it himself. Bear experts aren't sure why it happens, but perhaps the sight of a cub running away triggers a male bear's urge to hunt.

4. **Bears are fairly antisocial animals. They usually live alone in an area called a "home range", or territory, where they look for food. A bear's home range can be over 600 square km, so you don't often see bears together.**

5. **Bears like space around them. When the bears come to the Falls, they try to keep their distance from each other. It's bear good manners. It's like you sitting at your own lunch table rather than plonking your bottom on your teacher's sandwiches.**

Later

By the time we left, the sun had buried itself in a fluffy bed of afternoon clouds. Everyone was feeling tired but happy, and I guess that included the bears.

This evening we gathered in the cook shack to heat up our freeze-dried food and swap stories about the bears we saw. There was a buzz of excited voices.

"The bears were incredible!" I said to Jack. "This just has to be the most exciting day of my life!"

Jack looked up from his bowl of dry Grainy Crunch cereal and shrugged.

"It ain't just the sight of a lifetime, it's the sight of any number of lifetimes! There are plenty of bears at McNeil River each summer but elsewhere they're darn hard to spot! I've trekked three weeks in Montana without seeing a single bear. You've been here one day and you've seen dozens of the critters."

I asked Jack why there were so many bears at McNeil River.

"Fishing," said Jack, spraying me with his mouthful of Grainy Crunch.

I waited for him to finish his meal, and then asked why the fishing is so good.

BEN'S BEAR NOTES

FISH, BEARS AND WATERFALLS

I'VE GOT TO GET BACK!

1. Imagine a salmon that hatches from an egg in the McNeil River. The fish swims to the Pacific Ocean and for five years everything's fine. Then, one day, the salmon gets an overwhelming urge to go back to McNeil River. It wants to mate and (since it's a female) lay eggs.

2. Salmon aren't too smart but this is

definitely the most stupid idea our salmon's ever had. It will have to battle against the current of the river and jump waterfalls on the way. And it runs the risk of getting eaten by a hungry bear.

3. When the returning salmon reach the waterfalls they all get stuck in a salmon traffic jam. And that's why the bears find them so easy to catch.

4. The salmon that get past the bears end up in a bad way. They're worn out and bashed about by the rocks. The salmon mate and die, and the bears feast on their battered bodies.

Well, it's certainly been a long day. As I'm writing this I can't help wondering what tomorrow will bring. Will I find a bear cub to write about? What will happen to the bear cub? And will the mosquitoes finally manage to suck *all* my blood?

GRIZZLY GAMES FOR BAD BEAR CUBS

July 1

I'm pleased to report that I slept like a top – or is it a log? If I had a wooden head I couldn't have slept more soundly. Mind you, if I *did* have a wooden head at least I'd be safe from the bugs!

This morning I felt like a vampire's victim. I counted 20 itchy bites on my face and arms and hands and legs. And how did the little rascals get up my trouser-legs anyway? After a good scratch I sprayed myself all over with anti-mosquito spray. And then I did it three more times just to be on the safe side!

Well, Jack and I have been out to the Falls and today's big news is ... BEN'S FOUND A BEAR CUB FOR HIS DIARY!

OK, to be honest the bear cub found me. This afternoon we were standing on the upper viewing place. Jack leaned towards me. "Stand still," he whispered, "you've got a bear behind you!"

I thought he was joking. "Bare behind" get it? Then I looked at Jack's face and knew he was serious.

Nervously, I peered over my shoulder. A honey-coloured bear was watching us from some bushes close by. But she just stood there like she'd seen it all before.

"That's Honey," said Jack. "She's a regular visitor to the Falls. Can you see her cubs? The straw-coloured one's the girl cub – but the good-looking fella is the boy. He's quite something!"

And there, in the bushes, were the cubs.

The cubs were no bigger than large dogs. The boy cub was as fair as his sister but he had a whitish snout and a silver furry collar. He looked at me with his dark, shiny eyes, and I could see his wet black nose. His coat was damp and stringy and his ears stood up, a sign he was scared.

"Oh yes! Look at that little fellow," I whispered excitedly to Jack. "He's the one! He's the bear I'm going to write about." I didn't need to think about it.

The boy cub crept behind Honey and peeped out over her honey-coloured back. Then his sister stuck out her tan-coloured paw and thumped him on the nose. All at once the two little bears ran out of the bushes and started whacking each other.

ROCKY AND SANDY'S BOXING MATCH

"He's like that famous boxer – what's his name – Rocky!" Jack laughed.

"Yes," I agreed. "Rocky – I like that name! That's what I'll call him."

"So what will you call his sister?" asked Jack.

I sucked in my breath and frowned. Just then the cub in question fell over with a splat on a sandy patch of dirt. "She's chosen it herself!" I cried. "I'm going to call her Sandy."

"Hey – I get it!" said Jack.

"And it suits her colour!" I added.

"Well," Jack said, "I see you've found your cub. But take care you don't get too attached to him. It's real easy to get fond of a cub, but it's a heartbreak if it dies."

That's Jack. Always looking at the world through gloomy glasses. But maybe as a bear expert he knows a thing or two. Time will tell if he's right.

As we were talking, Rocky whacked his sister on the backside. "Ha ha – got you!" I imagined him shouting. Then Sandy bit her brother's leg and the two cubs rolled together on the grass.

We watched the cubs chase and scuffle until they were both worn out. Sandy crept back to Honey and snuggled under her chin, and Rocky nibbled grass shoots nearby. By then it was too late to talk about the dangers of getting too fond of a bear cub – I was bonded, glued and hooked for ever.

July 2

I'm back in my tent now after another day at the Falls. Jack's been telling me what he knows about Rocky and Sandy. He doesn't know all the details of their lives but he's enough of an expert to guess the bits he doesn't know. I've decided to turn Jack's information into a story…

Rocky and Sandy: the story so far...

Rocky and Sandy were born in January last year. As the winter snow piled up and the icy wind whistled outside, Honey was fast asleep in a sleeping hole, known as a "den". When the time came for the cubs to be born, Honey stirred and woke up just long enough to help her babies into the world. Then she fell back into a long, deep sleep.

The new-born cubs were no bigger than squirrels. They didn't have much fur and they couldn't see or hear. Somehow, they sniffed their way to Honey's tummy and fed on her rich gloopy milk.

Honey didn't wake up again until April. When she next opened her eyes she felt grumpy and dozy and only half-awake. Just think how grumpy certain humans get after eight hours of sleep. But Honey had slept for nearly seven months! Slowly, Honey shuffled to the den's entrance and peered outside. The snow still lay deep and crisp and white. "Oh drat!" thought Honey. "It's still winter!" She turned round and plodded back to her warm bed of leaves and moss.

OH NO, SNOW!

After a few days, Honey took another look outside, and every few days after that she would venture a little farther. At last she let her cubs take their first look at the world. Rocky and Sandy had fur now, and they could see, but they weighed less than a new-born human baby. I expect they were amazed to see sunshine and the funny, icy, white stuff we call "snow".

These were dangerous days for Rocky and Sandy. There was little food after the winter. Honey looked for last year's berries and the spring's new plant shoots to eat. Maybe she found a mouldy dead moose that had been covered by snow all winter. If there wasn't enough food, the bear family could die of hunger.

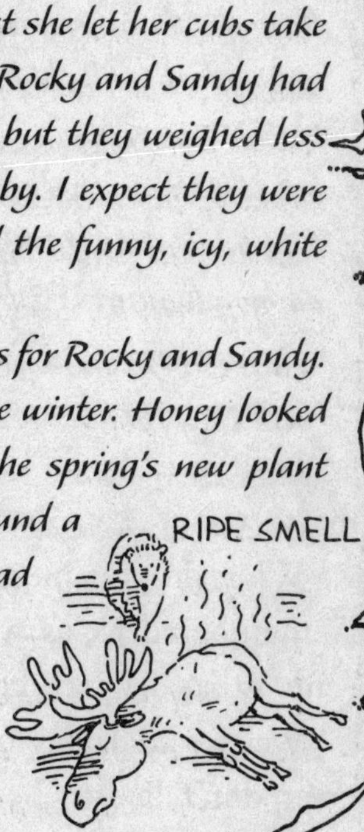

RIPE SMELL

Somehow, the cubs made it through the spring. Last summer Honey brought the cubs to McNeil River – the place she's visited in each of the ten summers of her life. That's where Jack first saw the bear family. He says Rocky and Sandy spent their time watching Honey and trying to copy her.

And now the bear family are back after another winter's sleep. Once again, Honey will try to catch as many fish as she can to feed herself and her cubs. Rocky and Sandy have grown bigger and stronger and they'll be ready to play more roughly and explore further than they did last year. I can't tell you what will happen to the bear cubs – but I'm sure that they'll have many, many adventures this summer.

"If they make it!" added Jack when I read him my story.

"What do you mean?" I asked, as my heart sank. I remembered Jack's warning about getting fond of a cub. What did Jack know about my cub's chances?

"Well," said Jack, "over half the cubs at McNeil River don't live to be three." Then he reeled off a long list of dangers such as getting lost, starving to death and being swept away in rivers. In the end, Jack left me in no doubt – my cub, Rocky, faces a rocky future. Well, this is real life and in the wild you can't be sure of anything.

July 3

Today, Honey was fishing at the waterfall. The cubs were feeling bored so they took it in turns to chase each other along the beach. All at once they seemed to forget who was chasing who. The two cubs ran towards each other. "GET OUT OF MY WAY!" I imagined them shouting. But neither bear dodged the other. So they bumped together and fell over like two teddies tumbling from a toy cupboard.

In seconds the cubs were up on their hind legs. They were romping and wrestling with happy bear grins on their faces. I imagined them giggling and shouting: "BUT IT WAS MY TURN!" "NO, IT WAS MINE!" "FIBBER!" "CHEAT!" and then giggling some more.

Meanwhile, Honey was busy watching the rushing water for leaping fish. After a while she caught a fish in her jaws and started feeding hungrily. Then she turned and glared at the playful cubs as if to say, "Can't you kids behave? Mum's eating!"

Honey was so busy keeping the cubs in order that she didn't spot the raven. The big black bird flapped down, grabbed a scrap of the fish and took off before Honey could stop it.

When I got back to the camp I asked the rangers about some of the other creatures they'd seen around McNeil River:

BEN'S BEAR NOTES

MCNEIL RIVER ANIMALS

1. The rush of salmon in the river is good news for every fish-eating bird. There are always crowds of seagulls at the Falls, looking for any scraps of dead fish left by the bears. And ravens are common visitors too.

2. If you're lucky you might see an eagle swooping to grab a fish, but they're quite rare.

3. Wolves often explore the shores of the cove, looking for dead fish. They usually keep their distance from the bears at the Falls. Here's a photo Jack took last year.

July 4

The visitors went home today. I was sorry to wave them off since I'd made a few friends. But it's going to be like this all summer. There'll be lots of visitors coming and going, and me, Brett, Molly, Jack and the bears sticking around.

July 5

Today Jack and I have been talking about bear cub games. In his 20 years of watching bears, Jack's seen an amazing number of different bear games and I've decided to turn his info into a guide. You may even want to try them yourself!

BEN'S GUIDE TO BEAR GAMES

(Suitable for bear cubs of all ages and grown-up bears if they're in the right mood!)

1. THE SNOW SLEDGE GAME: You sit on a snowdrift and slide down the slope on your bottom. If there's no snow around try sliding down a grassy bank. If your mum's in a good mood she might even slide down with you!

WHEEEEEE!

2. CHASE AND WRESTLE: This is the all-time bear favourite! You need two players – a bear brother and sister will do just fine. Take it in turn to chase each other. When you catch the other player, you both stand up and have a wrestle.

GRRRRR!

3. THE WRESTLING GAME: To wrestle like a bear, put your paws on the other cub's shoulders and try to push them over. It's OK to bite your brother or sister's ear. You can win extra points for throwing your brother or sister into the river. (By the way, human cubs are banned from biting

their brother or sister's ears and definitely banned from throwing their brother or sister into the river!)

4. THE BOXING GAME: The rules are the same as wrestling, but this time you have to whack your brother or sister with your paw. You're not allowed to hit them hard but you can growl and pretend to be a big tough bear. In fact, there's a special prize for the best bear actor or actress!

5. THE MUDDY GAME: (Human cubs should wear old clothes for this!) First, find the biggest, muddiest puddle for miles around. Splash through the puddle at top speed, spraying muddy water all over your brother or sister. If the mud goes on your mum, you risk being whacked by her big furry paw (and that goes for human cubs too!).

6. STOP THE GAME! So you don't want to play any more? That's OK! All you do is stop playing. Your brother or sister will get the message after a while. If they don't, lie on your back with your ears sticking up. That means "I give in - so go away and stop pestering me!"

July 8

Today Rocky was playing a game that isn't in my bear games guide. He'd found a puddle on a rocky ledge. His little mouth was down on the water and he was blowing bubbles. The bubbles were plopping and popping round his mouth and he was trying to bite them.

Later we saw a bear cub lesson. Young bears learn everything from their mums. They learn what plants to eat and where to find food, and how to deal with other bears. I guess being a cub is like having your mum as your school teacher.

Honey led the cubs past the upper viewing place. She stopped a few metres from us and sniffed some wood. The cubs sniffed the wood too. Then Honey stood up to get a better view. First Rocky and then Sandy also stood up to look around. Just imagine three bears playing follow my leader.

The bears looked really funny. I put my scarf in my mouth to stop myself laughing out loud. That made me turn red, and I went on making muffled snorting sounds until Jack told me off because I might upset the bears.

July 10

I woke up feeling great. I felt ready for anything. I really said, "This is the first day of the rest of my life!"

Then I looked outside and saw it was raining.

OK, I thought, so maybe the rest of my life is going to be rather wet!

Actually, it turned out to be *very* wet. The rain became heavier and heavier. I could hear it beating and spitting and splatting and hissing on my tent like a mad rattlesnake. Chatting over breakfast, Jack and I agreed that it was probably a bad idea to go to the Falls. But we decided to go anyway.

The bears were standing around looking soaked and soggy. They weren't doing much fishing and their heavy fur coats looked dark and dripping. A freezing wind blew the rain into my face and I could scarcely see the bears at all.

"Don't they ever get cold?" I asked Jack through chattering teeth.

Jack shook his head. "Their problem ain't cold –

it's *heat*. Their coats are so thick and warm, they like to get wet to cool off."

I watched the bears and wished I was as warm and waterproof as they were. The wind blew the rain sideways in huge wet shivering sheets. Somehow the raindrops found their way down my neck and up my sleeves and down my trousers. By the time we got back to the rangers' cabin we were both so wet that we dripped puddles on the wooden floor.

Molly made us some coffee and Brett said, "Say, have you guys been swimming?"

Well, it certainly felt like it!

BEAR BEDS AND MUM SWAPPING

July 13

Today we saw Honey and the cubs trotting out from some bushes near the trail. Jack reckons Honey's got a day bed there. But I don't mean a bed with a quilt and brass bed-knobs…

Maybe I ought to tell you something about sleeping bears…

BEN'S BEAR NOTES

BEAR BEDS

1. Like me, bears love lots of sleep. But unlike me, they sleep during the day, as well as at night.

2. A bear makes a bed by scraping a hollow in the ground. In winter, they line it with leaves and moss. Some bears spend most of their day resting on their beds. Do you know anyone this lazy?

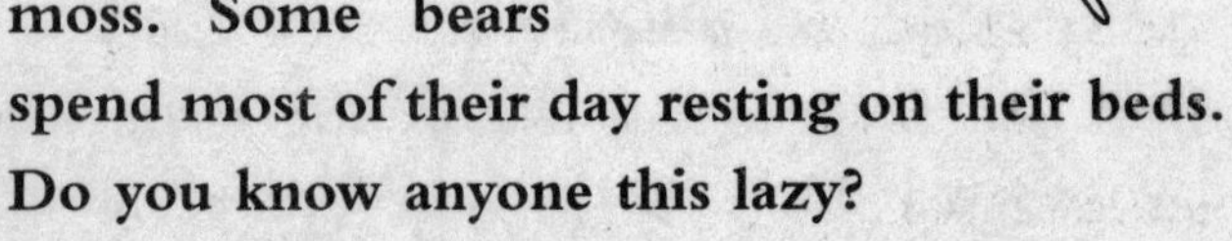

3. Bears have their main sleep when it gets dark (which is after 11 pm at present). They're early risers and they're usually out of bed and busily fishing before dawn. That's more than I could manage!

I wanted to take a peek at a sleeping bear but Jack says it can be really dangerous. Bears hate being woken or surprised by humans. Hmm, that's not surprising – I hate being woken up too.

July 16

It's amazing! I've been here more than two weeks and I've hardly said a word about the camp! I guess I've been much too excited about the bears. Anyway, here's everything you've ever wanted to know about life here – plus a few things besides!

A-Z OF MCNEIL COVE CAMP

A is for Awake at 6 am. It's already light and everyone is crawling out of their tents and yawning and stretching and grumbling about the cold.

B is for Breakfast. I usually have cereal and powdered milk.

C is for Cook Shack. It's where we eat breakfast and supper. We cook on an old wood-burning stove.

D is for Drinks. The water in the cook shack comes from a big can of rainwater. We have to filter the dirt out of the water and it takes for ever!

E is for Electricity. There's no electricity in the camp - so that means there's no TV, no computers, and no CD-players. On a more practical level, we have to do without a fridge, a washing-machine and electric heaters for those chilly nights.

F is for Food. All our food has to be stored in the cook shack so the bears won't steal it. I mostly eat freeze-dried and boil-it-up stuff.

G is for Grainy Crunch. Jack eats this cereal <u>without</u> milk. It doesn't look too tasty but Jack seems to like it.

H is for Home. That means my tent. It's blue and dome-shaped and it's so new it still smells new. Jack's tent is muddy and grubby and patched and weather-beaten. Like Jack, I expect the tent's had a few adventures.

I is for Ice. I dream of having a big tub of chocolate-chip ice cream with a gooey chocolate sauce all to myself. But the only ice around here is on the high mountains and there's no freezer in camp (see E for electricity).

J is for Juice. I'd also love some freshly squeezed orange juice with a wiggly straw, pleeeeeese.

K is for Coffee. (Sorry, I couldn't think of any "K" words!) Jack and I always have an evening cup at the rangers' cabin.

L is for Laundry. There isn't one round here and I'm having to wear smelly clothes. Yes, I could possibly wash some clothes in a bowl but it rains so much around here I'd never get them dry.

M is for Millions of Mosquitoes. There's millions of mosquitoes and each one wants to be my special friend. They're worse when the sun shines, but that isn't too often!

N is for Nights. They're usually cold and wet and windy.

O is for "Oh dear, last night my tent blew down!"

P is for Pegs. The tent pegs weren't very good at holding my tent in place.

Q is for Queue. There's always one of these to use the stove in the cook shack.

R is for Rocks. Jack showed me how to use rocks to weight down my tent. I'm hoping it won't blow down again!

S is for Sauna. This is a hot, steamy hut where you can sweat the dirt off your skin. You have to put wood in the stove to get it going and you make the steam from a bucket of pond water.

T is for Toilets. These are the outhouses hidden in the wet dripping bushes. They're smelly and basic inside!

U is for Underpants. My best pair of spotted

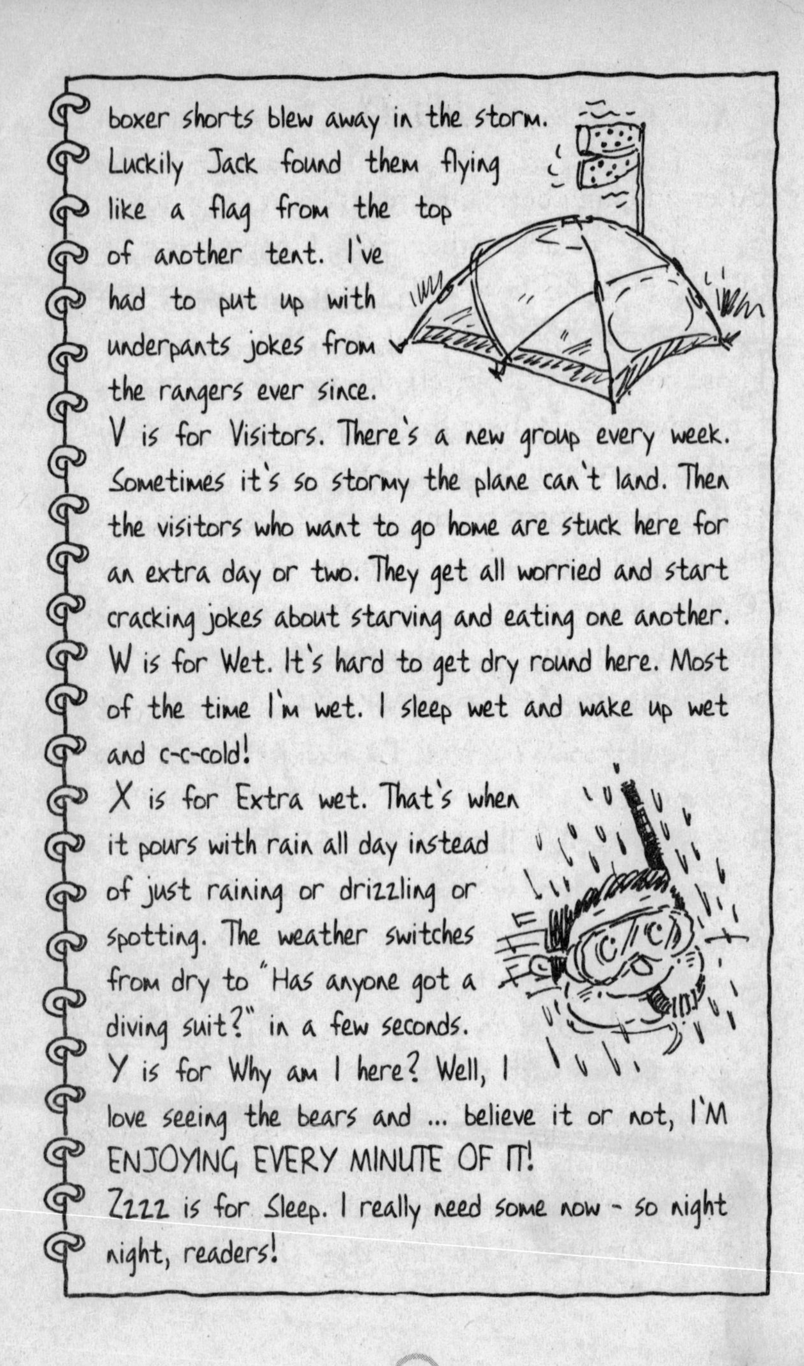

boxer shorts blew away in the storm. Luckily Jack found them flying like a flag from the top of another tent. I've had to put up with underpants jokes from the rangers ever since.

V is for Visitors. There's a new group every week. Sometimes it's so stormy the plane can't land. Then the visitors who want to go home are stuck here for an extra day or two. They get all worried and start cracking jokes about starving and eating one another.

W is for Wet. It's hard to get dry round here. Most of the time I'm wet. I sleep wet and wake up wet and c-c-cold!

X is for Extra wet. That's when it pours with rain all day instead of just raining or drizzling or spotting. The weather switches from dry to "Has anyone got a diving suit?" in a few seconds.

Y is for Why am I here? Well, I love seeing the bears and ... believe it or not, I'M ENJOYING EVERY MINUTE OF IT!

Zzzz is for Sleep. I really need some now - so night night, readers!

July 19

After watching bears for a few days, it's easy to think you know all about them. Yes, I know bears, you think, they're big furry balls of muscles and claws that plod around making bear noises. But in fact there's more to bears than meets the eye. For starters, did you know every bear has its own bear personality with its own little habits and ways?

I've been watching the male bears fishing across the Falls. There's three of them. I'm calling them Greedy, Lazy and Sneaky. They're not very nice names but they're really spot-on for these bears...

Greedy is a chocolate-brown bear. He's the largest of the three. He always grabs the best fishing space and he's *always* hungry. Yesterday I saw him catch 45 fish and his belly looked like three pillows stuffed into his bear coat.

Lazy is smaller and reddish brown. He gives up after about ten fish and ambles off into the bushes for a nice long nap. I think he feels it's too much like hard work.

Sneaky doesn't do much fishing. He *steals* his meals. He's smaller than Lazy, but he's bigger than the younger bears who fish downstream from the Falls. Every so often Sneaky creeps up on the younger bears, grabs one of their fish and wanders off. If he could talk he'd be saying, "Ssho longsh, shuckersh," with his mouth stuffed full of stolen fish.

Right at the end of the afternoon we spotted a new bear. It was a skinny youngster about four years old. The new bear was the clumsiest, scruffiest bear I'd ever seen. He had long legs and a long, raggedy, dirty brown coat, and he looked as if he was about to trip over his own paws. I've decided to call him Scruffy. Scruffy was hanging about on the same part of the beach as Rocky and Sandy.

Honey was fishing, but after a while the young male went too close to the cubs. Honey turned and growled and showed her teeth, but she didn't attack him. Maybe she sensed that the young male didn't mean any harm. Anyway, the growl was enough to scare off Scruffy. He lowered his head and slunk into the bushes to hide.

BEN'S BEAR NOTES

BEAR BODY LANGUAGE

1. Bears use their bodies to send signals to other bears. These signals help to sort out which bear is the boss and which bear should back down without a fight.

2. A bear that wants to show how tough it is will bare its teeth. A bear that doesn't want to fight will turn its head to one side or lower

its head. Growling is a sign that a bear is upset.

3. Sometimes bears charge an enemy but then stop before they attack. This is called a "mock charge". The bear wants to find out if their enemy will fight or run away. If the enemy runs, the bear will attack. But if the enemy stands their ground, the charging bear may decide to give up.

July 20

This evening Jack and I were sitting in the cook shack while the rain hammered down on the roof. We were warm and snug and the kettle was whistling on the wood-burning stove.

"I'm real thrilled, Ben," Jack said for about the tenth time.

"You said that two minutes ago," I reminded him.

"I know," he said, "but the fact that Honey came so close to us shows she's feeling more comfortable with people." Jack was talking about something that happened earlier today…

This afternoon Honey had led the cubs up the slippery slope towards the upper viewing place, which was just where we happened to be! It was thrilling – we could hear the cubs making funny little bleating sounds, like baby lambs.

"That means 'feed me'," whispered Jack.

Honey got the message. She crouched and then rolled onto her back and the cubs jumped on their mother's tummy. As usual Rocky went to his mum's left, and Sandy went to her right. Then they both made purring, happy bear cub sounds as they slurped the thick, gooey milk.

HONEY FEEDS HER CUBS

The bears were just three metres away. They were so close I could smell the soggy doggy whiff of their wet fur. Honey closed her eyes and waited for them to finish. Six minutes later the cubs had fed enough and were bouncing about again. Rocky was trying to swat Honey's face with his paw and Sandy had a little dribble of milk stuck to her nose. Suddenly, Honey stood up and the cubs squealed excitedly as they tumbled to the ground.

BEN'S BEAR NOTES

FEEDING BABY BEARS

1. New-born cubs are much smaller than their mums. If a human baby was this tiny compared to its mum, it would be the size of a walnut.

2. The fat-rich milk helps the cubs grow fast. Although the cubs eat other foods from about four months, they'll drink their mum's milk until they're about three.

3. After feeding, the mother and cubs often take a nap together.

Some of the mother bears take their cubs into the bushes to feed them. But as Jack says, Honey must be getting used to being near people. As for me, I feel really glad that the bears trust me enough to let me watch them feed.

July 25

Rocky and Sandy have made friends with two light-brown cubs. Their mum is a toffee-coloured bear so I'm calling her Toffee.

Jack said bear cubs may play with other cubs but they're not too happy playing with bigger bears. McNeil Falls is like a playground where the little kids are scared to play with big, rough kids. Luckily, Toffee's cubs are about the same size as Rocky and Sandy. We reckon they're the same age.

The four cubs looked as if they were having loads of fun, romping and wrestling on the beach. But Jack frowned. He said that Rocky and Sandy might wander too far and get lost. It sounds weird – but they could even end up with Toffee as their mum!

"It's rare, but it's happened before at McNeil Falls," said Jack with a frown as he tugged at his beard. "Cubs play together but sometimes they go off with the wrong mum. It's as if the cubs decide to swap mums!"

"That sounds cool!" I laughed. I remembered how, when I was a kid, I used to dream of swapping mums with my friends. I always wanted a really funky mum – the sort of mum who looked like a supermodel and bought me ice cream every day.

Jack shook his head. "Sometimes it works out," he said, "but the old mum can attack the new mum or the new mum can suddenly turn on the cubs and kill them – no one knows why."

"There you go, Jack," I thought. "Always taking the gloomy view!"

July 26

Er, actually Jack was right to be gloomy. Today things turned nasty for the bears.

Everything seemed fine as we watched the four cubs playing together. The cubs were taking it in turns to scamper after Toffee to beg for a scrap of the fish she'd just caught.

Honey always likes to know where her cubs are – even when she's fishing. But the next time she looked round, she couldn't see them. Neither could we – the cubs had gone!

Honey began to pant. Then she made a "WOOF" sound. I could see she was upset and I knew that she was calling her cubs. But there was no sign of them. Perhaps they were lost! A cold, terrible, helpless feeling swept over me. It was fear. I knew that a lost cub stood less chance than an ice lolly in a volcano.

BEN'S BEAR NOTES

LOST CUBS

1. Bear cubs under the age of three can't live without their mother. They're too young to find or catch food and they need their mum's milk to keep them going.

2. If a bear cub loses its mum, it soon feels scared. The cub makes panting, huffing or barking sounds to tell its mum where it is. The mother bear makes these sounds too, and a "WOOF" call to tell the cub to come to her.

3. The mother bear will use her hearing and sense of smell to track down the cub. They are very good at finding their cubs, even if it takes a day or two.

4. A lost bear cub is in terrible danger. If its mother doesn't find it, it might easily starve or be killed by a big male bear.

Desperately, Honey started to sniff her way along the stony shore in search of her cubs' scent. Every so often she gave a worried pant or "WOOF".

Jack shook his head. "It's no good," he said sadly. "I guess the puddles are hiding the smell and she can't hear anything over the sound of the waterfall."

Jack was right – 20 minutes later, Honey was still searching for her cubs. Then, suddenly and without warning, Jack gripped my arm hard.

"OUCH!" I cried.

"Look over there!" said Jack, pointing excitedly. "It's the cubs!"

"Yes!" I exclaimed. "I can see them now!"

Sure enough, the cubs were on the beach about 200 metres away. But there was a heap of boulders between the cubs and Honey. She'd never be able to see them!

But then Honey stood up. To see Honey up on her hind legs is an awesome sight – she's as tall as me.

"Honey's trying to get a scent from the air," said Jack. "But I figure that won't help her much. Look!"

Rocky and Sandy had run off to join Toffee's cubs, who were splashing about in a little stream.

"Oh no!" I cried. "They're running even further away!"

But Honey was still on her hind legs and she had a good view of the stream. As soon as Honey saw her cubs, she bounded towards them.

Toffee's cubs saw Honey and started barking in fear. Toffee whipped around and tore towards Honey. The two mother bears slowed to a slow-motion walk as they got closer. They snarled and growled but they didn't fight. Toffee didn't want to take on Honey. She dropped her head and slunk away.

Honey led Rocky and Sandy up the path towards our viewing place. At the top, she stopped and licked their faces crossly with her rough slurpy tongue.

She seemed to be telling them, "And don't you *ever* run off like that again!" Then she rolled onto her back and gave them both a lovely big feed of milk.

For the rest of the day Honey kept an extra-close watch on Rocky and Sandy. She made them stay on the rocky ledge where she was fishing. And when Rocky tried to get down, Honey fetched him back with a woof, and gave him a big wallop with her paw. Jack said bear mums sometimes whack their cubs when they're naughty. Well, after everything that's happened today, I could see why Honey was so strict. The cubs really do live on the edge. I just wonder what sort of trouble they'll be in next. And will they be so lucky next time?

BREAKFAST WITH BEARS

July 30

OH NO! It was half-past eight, I was late for school and I couldn't find my trousers!

I was half dressed before I realized I'd been dreaming. I was a long way from school and it was only four o'clock in the morning! But it was already light and, for once, the sun was shining. The air was calm and clear and the mountains across the cove looked close enough to touch.

I made up my mind to take a little stroll along the beach. Not very far – just a little way towards the sedge field. I was the only person awake. It was so quiet I could hear myself breathing. The only other sounds were the gentle breeze whispering in the bushes and the slurpity-slurp of tiny waves licking the beach. Just then I heard an eagle's screech from across the water.

It was so beautiful I felt tingly all over.

In the distance I spotted three bears. They were a long way ahead of me, but fortunately I'd brought my binoculars. I took a good look at them. The larger bear was Honey. The two smaller bears romping around at her heels had to be Rocky and Sandy. I wondered if the bears would notice me. At least the wind was blowing on my face so there was no way they could sniff my scent.

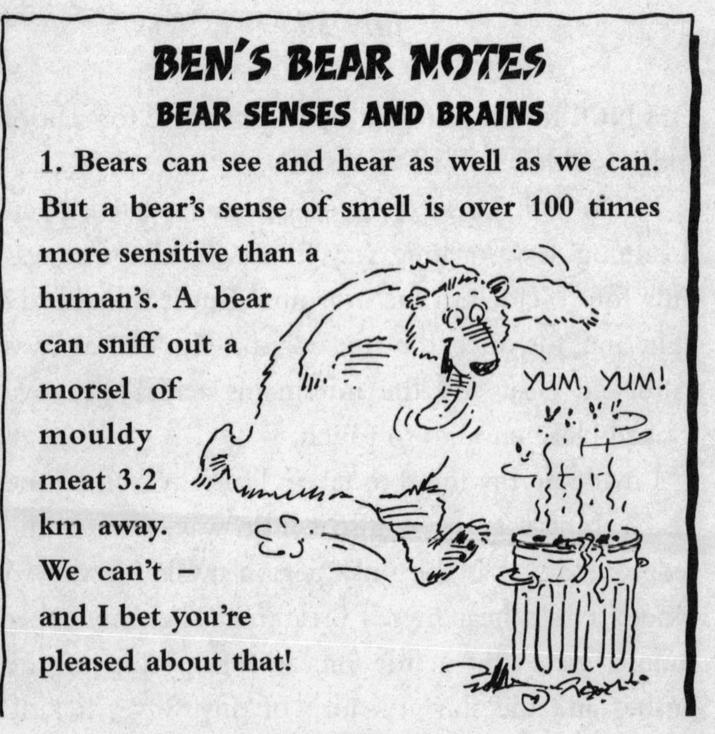

BEN'S BEAR NOTES

BEAR SENSES AND BRAINS

1. Bears can see and hear as well as we can. But a bear's sense of smell is over 100 times more sensitive than a human's. A bear can sniff out a morsel of mouldy meat 3.2 km away. We can't – and I bet you're pleased about that!

2. Bears are smart animals. If a bear thinks it's being followed by a human, it tries to shake them off. The bear might jump from rock to rock so it doesn't leave paw-prints in the mud.

3. If a bear's in a bad mood, it might decide to attack the human. Some bears circle round behind a hunter and wait in ambush.

Twenty minutes later I'd managed to creep 200 metres closer. The bears had stopped for a munch of sedge plants. I couldn't see them too well because the sedge has grown really long in the past few weeks. All I could see was Honey's back and the heads of the cubs with their small furry ears.

Just then I spotted another bear. It was trotting along the beach towards Honey and the cubs. I peered through my binoculars. It looked like ... YES! I was sure of it! It was Scruffy.

Honey gave Scruffy a warning look. "Go away!" she seemed to be telling him. Poor Scruffy beat a hasty retreat. A few minutes later he spotted a big male bear on the other side of Mikfik Creek. The big bear might have been Greedy but he was too far away for me to be sure. Scruffy panicked and ran back towards Honey. Suddenly he stopped. "Er, wait a minute," I imagined him thinking, "I can't go this way either!" So he crept into some bushes to hide.

Meanwhile, Honey had spotted the big male. She watched him carefully, but luckily he hadn't seen her yet. He was busily looking for dead fish that had been washed down the creek. The breeze was blowing the big bear's scent towards Honey, and stopping him from getting a sniff of her and the cubs. But just to be safe, Honey decided to lead the cubs back along the beach. This meant they were heading my way!

OH NO, OH NO, OH NO! I thought. If Honey gets much closer, she's going to see me!

I'd wandered a long way from camp. If Honey turned nasty, I was on my own. This time I was really in the soup.

"Never run from a bear!" The advice rang through my racing brain like a fire alarm bell. But what could I do? I stood still as I tried to figure out a plan.

As it turned out, doing nothing was the best move. Luckily, Honey spotted a dead fish down by the water and she and the cubs went to take a look. Sighing with relief, I backed towards the camp. Cold sweat trickled down my neck and my hands were shaking as if I'd seen a ghost.

From a safe distance I peered at the bears through my binoculars. Honey was munching the shiny dead fish. Rocky and Sandy were dancing around her, trying to grab their share. All the bears had red jaws and fish blood dripping from their mouths.

After a while I happened to glance at my watch. Oh no, I was late for breakfast! I knew I'd be missed and I knew I'd be in big trouble. I wasn't supposed to watch bears without Jack.

Jack was standing outside the rangers' cabin with his arms folded and a cross look on his face.

"So where did you get to?" he snapped. "We were about to send out a search party!"

"Sorry, Jack," I said in a small voice. Then I crept wretchedly back to my tent, feeling like Scruffy when he was scared off by the big bear. What a rotten end to a lovely morning!

August 2

I've never seen so many bears at the Falls. Today Jack and I counted 60, and more bears are turning up every day. Even I can work out why the bears are coming here. The Falls are jumping with more fish than ever. It's a bear's dream summer holiday! If bears had travel agents, I bet they'd all be selling tickets.

I've spent most of the day watching an old bear whom I'm calling Grizzle.

Jack says Grizzle's the oldest bear at the Falls and she's been seen coming here for 20 years. Wild bears live about 25 years and you can see old Grizzle is getting on a bit. Her claws are blunt and her eyes are cloudy. Grizzle walks in a stiff, slow way and sways from side to side as if she's aching. She's like an old lady with bad hips. You can imagine her grumbling to herself and saying, "Things were better in my day!"

August 7

Today I thought I'd write about bear's eating habits. Like me, the bears eat their lunch standing up. But I eat peanut butter sandwiches and the bears eat raw fish. I wouldn't swap my sandwiches for one of the bear's fish – especially not a fish with its head on and its glassy dead eyes staring sadly as you eat it.

After lunch Honey scrambled onto her favourite rock and looked down at the whooshing water. Rocky and Sandy crouched beside her. Suddenly a fish leaped from the water and Honey caught it in her mouth. I could see the big silvery salmon flipping and flapping in her jaws.

An hour later

Honey caught six fish in the last hour. Not bad, eh? But then she began to get a little fussy in her eating habits. Jack said the bits of fish that give a bear the most energy are the brains, the skin and the eggs. And guess which bits Honey was eating?

She ripped a little hole in the salmon's side with her curved claw and squashed the body with her big heavy paw. It was gross! A splurge of splattering, slithering, orange fish eggs squirted out like the insides of an over-squishy mango.

"Nice trick with the claws, huh?" said Jack.

"They remind me of extra-long fingernails," I replied. Mind you, my fingernails would only be that long if I let them grow for FIVE whole years!

Jack looked at me seriously and nodded.

"I hadn't thought of it that way! But bears use claws like we use our nails. A bear can pick a peanut from a crack in the plaster with its claws."

Whilst we were talking, the bear family was lapping and slurping at the gloopy fish eggs. Rocky raised his little head and let out a big, happy burp. Then Honey ripped open the salmon's shiny scaly skin and pulled it off. It's like me rolling a sock off my pink sweaty foot with my teeth! I don't even want to think about trying this trick on Jack...

Afterwards the cubs enjoyed a bit of bear fisticuffs (or should that be paw-cuffs?) over the remains of the skinless salmon. But Honey stuck her big head between them and crunched the salmon's skull to get at its battered brains.

I'd left one of my sandwiches to eat later – but I didn't want it any more!

August 10

Today Rocky trotted along the shore and headed straight towards us. He stopped just a couple of metres away – if he'd come any closer I could have touched him! But it was an awkward moment because Honey was giving us a nasty look.

Rocky sniffed my wading boots. As usual I'd left them out to dry after they'd got wet wading across the creek. Then Rocky began to *chew* one of my boots!

"Don't stop him!" whispered Jack. "We never disturb the bears here, whatever they get up to."

At that moment Honey barked and Rocky scampered back to her. But he left my boot covered in little holes and bear dribble.

Er, thanks, Rocky! My badly bear-bitten boot leaked ice-cold water as I crossed the creek in the afternoon. My socks made soggy squelching sounds all the way back to camp – and the walk felt a lot further in sopping soggy socks.

Anyway, Rocky's attempt to eat my wading boots made me wonder why bears always seem to be hungry.

BEN'S BEAR NOTES

FOOD, LOVELY FOOD!

1. Food is vital to bears. It's even more vital to bears than it is to me, and that's saying a lot! You see, bears have to eat through the summer to build up their fat reserves. The fat stores energy to keep the bears going through the winter when they are asleep.

2. Bears are especially hungry in the spring when they wake up from their winter sleep because they haven't eaten for more than six months. In the autumn, the bears sense that it's their last chance to feed before the winter and go into ultra-hungry mode. An adult

bear can eat 16 kg of food a day – that's equal to 100 doughnuts. Could you eat that?

3. Like humans, bears eat meat, fish and plants. Like us, they have pointy meat-eating (canine) teeth at the front of their mouths and plant-grinding teeth called molars at the back.

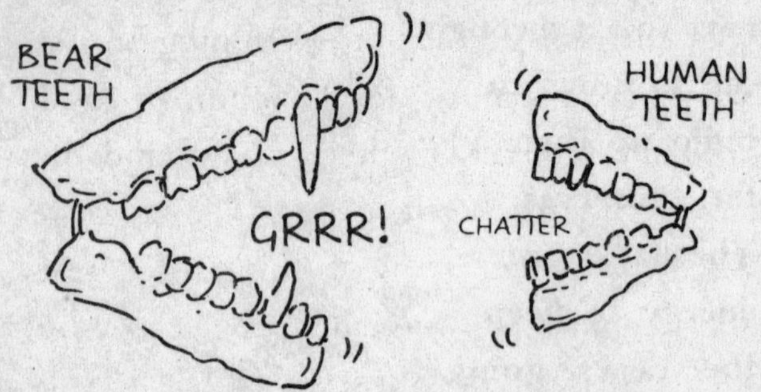

The main difference is that bear fangs are bigger than my little pointy teeth – and yours too, I hope!

Anyway, talking about bear fangs, I'd better whack some sticking plaster over those fang holes in my wading boots.

August 13

Last night I read my bear notes to the other visitors. Some of them laughed. Then Rita, who works at Yellowstone National Park, in Wyoming, said that bears at Yellowstone sometimes break into cars. They pinch picnics and they trash cars and even use them as a toilet. Hmm – they sound like bear burglars to me!

Well, that started everyone swapping bear stories.

"Bears are a bit too fond of human food," said Jack. "They remember where they found the food and they come back very determined to get more."

"So what other sort of things do bears like eating?" I asked as I munched my heated-up spicy noodle surprise. (The "surprise" is that it tastes even worse than it smells.)

"What *don't* they eat?" said Jack, laughing. "Bears ain't too fussy."

Then, helped by Molly and Brett, he came up with a list of bear treats that I found really suprising. Some of these foods sound even worse than spicy noodle surprise!

The Brown Bear Good Food Guide

THE BEST PLACES FOR BEARS TO EAT BREAKFAST, LUNCH AND DINNER

WILD SALAD BARS: Bears love greens but they only like juicy tender shoots and leaves. Their guts can't deal with tough old stringy stuff. Smart salad snack bars for starving bears are patches of wild celery, wild rhubarb, and dandelions – and they'll happily raid human gardens.

FISH DINERS: For any hungry bear, McNeil River is the best fish diner in Alaska.

MOOSE MEAT CARVERY: Bears will eat a moose whenever they get the chance – but that's not too often. A moose can run further and faster than a bear. The best moose carvery is a moose that's been killed by wolves. Hungry bears chase away the wolves and help themselves to the moose meat! If they can't find fresh meat they sniff out smelly rotten moose or elk bodies – the juicy maggots really add to the ripe flavour – yum yum!

FURRY NIBBLES: Little furry animals make a tasty snack. Brainy bears know how to dig out dinner at marmot or mice burrows.

TINY SNACK BARS: Fat, squirming wasp and grasshopper grubs make a quick snack. And there are live ants for bears who don't mind a squirt of ant acid on their tongues.

SWEET TREATS: Bears love sweet sticky foods. The best bear dessert diners are berry patches in the autumn. Finally, for a bit of bear heaven, bears make a beeline for their nearest bee's nest. Honeycomb with juicy bee grubs gives a real buzz to a hungry bear!

So there you are – bears really aren't too fussy. In fact, Jack tells me that bears have even been known to snack on seat padding, dine on dynamite and breakfast on battery acid! So are you a fussy eater? Well, if you hate school-dinner custard, and slimy green sprouts make you heave, you'll be shocked to know that a bear will eat both. Yes, custard and sprouts mixed up together with cold, greasy chips thrown in!

August 15

Rocky is getting cheeky. *Much* too cheeky, if you ask me!

Today he sneaked up on me at the lower viewing place. I was busy watching Honey fishing and I didn't notice Rocky. The sun had come out after a wet start, and I'd left my gloves on the ground to dry.

Next thing I knew, Rocky was beside me, grunting happily as he chewed my glove. He was so close I caught the scent of his warm, woody-smelling fur.

As soon as I saw him I shouted, "HEY, ROCKY! THAT'S MY GLOVE!"

And do you know what that naughty cub did? He only ran off with my glove in his mouth! Sandy, who'd been watching from a safe distance, joined in the chase. She grabbed the glove in her teeth and dashed behind some rocks with it. And that was the last I ever saw of my glove.

I'm writing this with a cold hand.

August 17

Here's a hard bear question. What's the link between:

a) Bears

b) Tuna fish

Any ideas?

Well, you might say that bears will eat your tuna sandwiches, along with the rest of your picnic. But that isn't the answer I was looking for. And being a teacher I'll only give a mark for the correct answer.

D'you give up?

Well, BEARS and TUNA both eat SALMON. But if the tuna scoff too many salmon there won't be enough for the bears. And if the bears snack on too many salmon, not enough will live to lay eggs, so there'll be fewer young salmon for the tuna's tea. And if there's less for the tuna to eat, they'll starve, and there'll be less tuna in your sandwich! Hold on, this is getting rather complicated…

BEN'S BEAR NOTES

FOOD WEBS

1. Plants and animals all depend on one another for food. Even two animals that never eat one another may depend for food on a third animal that they both eat. Scientists call this a "food web".

2. A food web is a bit like a spider's web, only there are lots of animals in it – and it's nothing to do with catching flies. Here's a food web for an Alaskan brown bear:

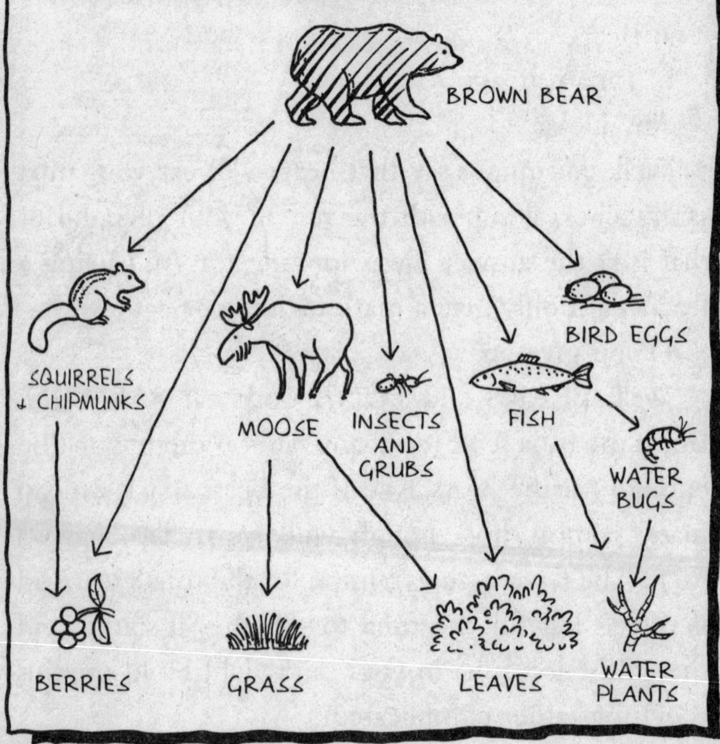

August 20

The nights are getting darker. Well, a bit. It's still no darker than twilight for most of the night. But the twilight is more gloomy and shadowy and colder than a few weeks ago. And I know this to my cost. Today you're in for a tale that will make you glad you're living in a nice warm home with an indoor toilet.

One of the hardest things to do round here is to get to the toilet at night. When you wake up in the night I can guarantee that you won't be able to find your torch. So you try to find your way blindly along the muddy, ankle-twisting path around the tents. It starts to rain. You find the toilet – HURRAH! But now you've forgotten where your tent is! You trip over one or two tent guy ropes and fall on your face. By the time you find your tent, you're tired and muddy and cold and wet. In fact, you're so cold and wet that you want to go to the toilet again!

BATH-TIME WITH BEARS

August 24

Now I bet you're wondering how I keep clean. I wonder myself sometimes! Washing is actually one of the hardest things to do around here. The camp has no baths and no showers – not even a water tap.

Jack and I take it in turns to fetch water from a stream a few hundred metres away. But that's easier said than done. Our ten-gallon water container is really heavy and the further you have to drag it, the heavier it feels.

And washing in cold water is no fun. I want to shriek "EEK!" as the icy drops trickle down my neck. The water's so cold, just *thinking* about it makes me shiver.

The only hot way to get clean is the sauna. But this evening I tried to take a sauna and ended up sharing my bath with two bears. Here's what happened…

There I was, enjoying my hot steamy sauna. Actually the sauna felt hotter than hot. Imagine feeling so hot that your skin glows bright red and your head feels like a plum in a plum pudding. Imagine feeling so hot that your guts gurgle like hot pipes and your legs are heavy with heat. This is GREAT – after a day of watching bears in the wet and cold, it feels heavenly to be hot.

But then my peaceful session in the sauna was shattered. I heard sounds. I could make out heavy breathing and I knew there was someone – or something – outside the door. Whatever it was, it was BIG. So I thought maybe it was Walt (he's a rather overweight visitor).

But no. These were bear sounds! There was no mistaking it – *there was a big bear prowling around outside the sauna hut*. A cold shiver ran down my back. Come to think of it, I was boiling hot – so it was more of a hot shiver.

Alarm bells jangled between my ears. "PANIC STATIONS!" shouted my brain. And my heart played a dramatic drum-beat. Meanwhile, sweat was running down my face like a waterfall.

Then came a CRASH! as a heavy paw whacked against the door. I heard loud panting outside. Then came some more panting – GASP, GASP, GASP – but that was just from me!

I froze with fear. Well, maybe "froze" isn't the right word. I felt as if I was *melting* into a sticky goo like an ice cream in an oven. I didn't dare breathe, so after a while I started to turn purple.

Silence.

Then I made out the noise of the bear breathing but it sounded further away. Maybe it had moved off. But why hadn't anyone raised the alarm? Had no one spotted the bear?

"Woof!" barked the bear. It sounded even further away. I knew I had to warn the rest of the camp and get help fast.

So I tiptoed to the door and opened it a teeny-tiny crack. I could just see Honey heading away from the hut. Rocky and Sandy must be close by.

"How can my bears do this?" I said. Was this some kind of cruel bear joke they were playing on me? Well, it wasn't funny!

"Time to make a break!" I thought.

I grabbed my towel, wrapped it around my middle, and crept from the hut. But disaster struck! Suddenly an icy blast of wind made me hop like a chilly kangaroo. The wind made the towel flap about my tummy. Honey saw the movement and stared at me.

My heart stopped. Luckily, bears aren't too upset by nearly nude teachers with knobbly knees. Rocky and Sandy even stood up on their hind legs to get a better view.

I dodged behind the hut. But that was a BIG MISTAKE! Now I was heading away from the camp – away from safety. But my feet had their own plan and that plan was to run for it. Trouble was, my feet were too fast for my own good. My towel caught on a scratchy branch and my foot caught on a piece of dead wood. I tumbled head over heels and landed with a big SPLOSH in the smelly green pond.

Moments ago I'd been too hot. Now I was too cold. Wet, scummy, muddy, and shivering with cold. There was pond water in my eyes and pond water in my ears and something like frogspawn up my nose. I sat miserably in the muddy water, dressed in strings of slimy weed.

The bears were staring at me as if I'd just landed from Mars. But the cubs decided that ponds were fun. All at once they leaped into the water to join me. Rocky sat in the pond and whacked water at my face. Sandy found a water lily and started chewing it.

Then I heard someone shouting, "I'VE FOUND HIM!" It was Walt. Walt stared open mouthed at me and the bears.

"Is Ben OK?" called Brett from the rangers' cabin.

"He's fine," yelled Walt. "He's just taking a bath with some bears!"

"Get me a towel!" I wailed.

"Now he wants his towel!" shouted Walt. "I bet he wants some shampoo too!"

"No thanks," I whimpered.

But then Walt had an idea. "Hey, Ben! Do you mind if I grab a picture? I can't wait to show this to the folks back home." And guess what? He had his camera with him! As Walt pressed the button a big blob of pond slime dripped from my nose like thick green snot.

Half an hour later, I was in the rangers' cabin. I was wrapped in a blanket and holding a steaming mug of coffee. My teeth were chattering as I tried to explain how I came to be having a bath with two bears.

Just then Jack came in. He grinned at the sight of my muddy face.

"Hey, Ben, you're a mess!" he said, laughing. "Looks like you could use a wash. The sauna's free!"

August 26

I've been at McNeil River nearly two months!

"It only feels like two days," I said to Jack over breakfast.

"I know how you feel," said Jack. "But the bears have changed quite a lot in that time. Haven't you noticed?"

I shook my head. To my shame, I hadn't.

"Remember how the bears looked in June?" Jack asked.

I frowned and racked my brains to remember. "Well," I said, "I think their coats were longer and more straggly."

"Yep." Jack nodded. "Those were winter coats. The bears have grown summer coats now. They're kinda like summer clothes – thinner and cooler. What else?"

I tried to stretch my brain a bit further. "Honey and the cubs are looking a bit fatter," I suggested.

"I knew you could do it!" said Jack approvingly. "Back in June they were still quite skinny. Honey's been eating about 20 fish a day since then."

This afternoon I watched Grizzle, the old bear, fishing in Mikfik Creek. The bubbling, rushing water swished and splashed around her old legs. Like most old bears, Grizzle fishes slowly. She stood very still and only jumped on a fish when she was sure of catching it. Every move Grizzle made was the result of years of experience.

A few metres downstream, Scruffy was also staring at the water. But unlike Grizzle, Scruffy still has a lot to learn about fishing. He was so excited that he hopped from one leg to the other like a human who wants to go to the toilet. As soon as he spotted a fish, he belly-flopped into the water. The fish got away.

Scruffy missed nine fish. But on his tenth attempt he somehow managed to splash a big, shiny salmon onto the beach. He sniffed it in delight and started dancing around it. I could imagine him yelling, "HEY! LOOK AT ME – I'VE DONE IT! HA! HA! I FEEL GOOD!"

But the fish wriggled past Scruffy and plopped back into the river. Scruffy gazed at the river in horror. "OH SHUCKS!" he seemed to be thinking.

Jack says that young bears often get over-excited when they're fishing, while the older, more sensible bears get on with the job. If you ask me, they're a bit like children and teachers!

BEARS BEHAVING BADLY

August 28

We've been at the Falls since ten this morning and at first everything was much the same as usual. Honey was fishing. Rocky and Sandy were playing nearby. Every so often Honey fed her cubs. But about an hour ago things started happening. And happening very fast…

We first knew something was wrong when we spotted a big bear crashing through the bushes on the other side of the Falls. A *very* big bear. I hadn't seen him before and I watched him closely. The big bear had a dark shaggy coat and a long white scar on his nose.

When he saw the bear, Jack's face fell. He grabbed my arm so tightly it hurt.

"It's Slasher!" he hissed.

"*Slasher?*" I repeated stupidly.

Jack nodded and swallowed nervously. "Slasher's the biggest and fiercest bear along the McNeil River. The year before last he attacked another male for no reason at all!"

I gasped.

Slasher was acting like he owned the place. You could see he thought he was the boss by the way he walked. He didn't stop to look around or sniff the air like a smaller bear. He was afraid of nothing.

"Look at him!" exclaimed Jack. "He never plays like the other bears. He just prowls about pushing them around."

But even Jack didn't expect what happened next!

Slasher padded down to the Falls. All the other bears got out of his way. Greedy waddled off. Sneaky slunk away to hide and Lazy slouched into the nearest bushes. None of them was as big and mean-looking as Slasher.

Only one bear was left on Slasher's side of the Falls. Scruffy was still happily fishing. He didn't notice the big bear until he was only a few metres away. For a moment I thought that Slasher would attack Scruffy. Scruffy must have thought so too.

The younger bear was so scared he tried to jump clear but ended up falling into the fast-flowing river. Scruffy vanished for a few seconds before he managed to drag himself out and scuttle into the bushes.

But Slasher wasn't interested in Scruffy. He knew exactly where he was going. He was crossing the river to our side. We watched the big bear pushing through the rushing water as if it was a paddling pool.

"He makes it look easy," whispered Jack, "but that current is strong enough to sweep you or me away in a second."

When Honey saw Slasher coming towards her she became stressed. Her ears went flat and she began to back away, shielding her cubs with her body. The cubs were scared and they were barking with fear. Honey lowered her head to one side to show Slasher that she didn't want a fight.

But Slasher was on the beach now. He stared straight at Honey as if his eyes could drill holes in her. What could Honey do?

The mother bear stared back with dark, frightened eyes. Then she growled and bared her teeth. She's half scared and half angry now, I thought.

Slasher was snarling and I could see the foamy spit dripping from the corners of his big, twitching mouth. It was a sign of anger. He looked like a bad-tempered man working himself up into a terrible rage.

I shook Jack's arm. "What does Slasher want?" I asked urgently.

Jack tore his gaze away from the bears. He gave me a strained look.

"I dunno," he said tensely. "I've never seen anything like it. Honey's just trying to protect her cubs, but Slasher's getting too close!"

A moment later Slasher charged with huge bounding strides. For such a big bear, he moved very fast. Honey and the cubs stared in horror – they seemed stuck to the spot with superglue. A moment later Slasher smashed into Honey and the two bears were fighting.

"Can't we stop them?" I cried, stepping forward.

"Stay where you are!" ordered Jack.

I bunched my fists and bit my lip. Honey was

about half Slasher's size. It looked like she didn't stand a chance – but I knew she'd die fighting for her cubs.

Honey and Slasher tore at each other like crazy cats. In a matter of seconds they were on their hind legs, biting and clawing and grappling and growling. I remembered Rocky and Sandy playing like this – but this time the fight was for life or death.

All of a sudden, blood sprayed from Slasher's mouth. His lip was torn. The big dark bear bellowed as he dropped onto all fours and turned away. His head was down. Then Honey lowered her head too. The fight was over. And Honey had won!

I looked about me. I felt dazed and shaky, as if I'd been in a fight myself.

We watched the bears until it was time to go back. There was no more drama – thankfully! Honey,

Rocky and Sandy stayed on our side of the Falls. Honey glared at Slasher who had gone back across the river. The big bear was acting as if Honey wasn't there. He took the best fishing spot in the Falls and started fishing.

Tonight, everyone's been talking about the fight. The visitors saw the battle and some of them even filmed it. But what does it mean for Honey, Rocky and Sandy? Some visitors think that Slasher will attack again. Jack says it won't happen, but what if he's wrong? I'm really, *really* worried.

August 29

I went to the Falls today hoping against hope that the cubs were OK. And they were! Honey was fishing again, but she still looked edgy. She kept gazing around as if she was expecting to see Slasher charging towards her.

Today was an EXTRA WET day. It poured with rain and even the bears found it too wet to get much done. We stayed until the rising tide cut us off at Mikfik Creek. Brett, who'd been working in the rangers' cabin, came to fetch us in the camp's boat. When at last we slopped and dripped back into camp, we looked as if we'd escaped from some dreadful shipwreck.

August 30

What a TERRIBLE day. We've been at the Falls all day but there's no sign of Honey and the cubs anywhere. Until now the bear family have been at the Falls every day. Where have they got to? Has something happened to them?

The rain fell in wild, wet sheets. It rattled on the hood of my rain-jacket and soaked my diary until the soggy pages stuck together.

Jack nudged me. "Wanna know something?" he asked.

"What?" I replied grumpily, still looking for Honey and the cubs.

"Well," said Jack slowly, "there's no sign of Slasher."

I put two and two together and broke out in a cold sweat. "That's it!" I gasped. "Honey and the cubs have run away and Slasher's followed them."

"Hey, not so fast!" said Jack. "Bears don't do that kind of thing. The fight was a one-off. Most likely they've left for the winter – and it so happened to be the same day."

I shook my head crossly. How could I end my

diary with the bears going missing like this? There was only one thing we could do.

"We'll have to go after them," I said. "We've just got to!"

Later

Jack and I have been talking to the rangers. We've been trying to get them to agree to let us follow Honey and the cubs. But it hasn't been easy.

The candle on the table threw big black shadows on the walls of the rangers' cabin. Everyone looked tense. Jack's mouth drooped grimly. The shadows deepened the lines on his forehead and made him look years older.

"I don't know," said Molly for the tenth time. "We're kind of going outside our job here."

"But we're only going to be away for a few days," pleaded Jack. "All we wanna do is go after the bears and check out what happened to them."

Molly shook her head tiredly. "Bears are leaving the Falls all the time," she said. "It's going to be winter in a few weeks. The bears always leave about now to eat the ripe berries before the weather closes in."

I knew Molly had a point. It's only August, but each day it's getting dark seven minutes earlier. This far north it's already autumn and it'll be winter in a few weeks.

But Jack and I weren't going to take "no" for an answer. "Yeah, sure," said Jack. "But look at the timing – just after a fight."

"The cubs could be in danger!" I added.

Brett gripped his mug of coffee until his knuckles gleamed white. "I see you guys are set on it," he said. "But we can't make the final decision. I'll have to radio the bosses in Anchorage in the morning. Let's see what they say."

I went to sleep thinking about Jack. Why did he agree to follow the bears? Why is he so keen to find out what's happening? He's never actually said how he feels about the bears, but I guess he must really care about them, as any naturalist would.

September 1

The bosses didn't say "yes" or "no", they said, "Hmm ... maybe". Jack pushed a bit harder. He reminded them that he was a ranger and a bear expert. He said he knew where the bears were heading. Then he promised we wouldn't do anything to disturb the bears.

In the end the bosses gave in, but as Jack's supposed to be helping the other rangers, we've been given just a week to find the bears and get back to camp.

Today I've been packing my rucksack. This evening I asked Jack if he was serious about not disturbing the bears.

"Come what may, we can't get involved," he said.

"Not even to save their lives?" I asked.

Jack shook his head firmly. "I mean it," he said. "As a bear scientist I have to watch what happens. We've got to let the bears get on with their own lives."

September 2

We set off this morning. I've agreed to try the same food as Jack – dry Grainy Crunch, and strips of meat that Jack dried in the wind. These foods are light to carry and they don't smell, so we shouldn't have unwanted bears sniffing around. I tried a mouthful of dry cereal at lunchtime and thought, "Hey, where's the milk?" Then I thought, "Hey, where's the fruit and yoghurt to go with it?!"

At supper it was time to try the dried meat. Jack handed me a strip and I tried not to think of the flies that had crawled across it as it dried. I shut my eyes and chewed on a teeny-tiny morsel. It tasted of old dishcloths. The morsel got halfway down my throat and stuck there.

We had walked all day, up and over windswept hills with the rain beating in our faces. Jack says we're following a bear path. Bears follow the same path for years. In places like Kodiak Island, each bear steps in the actual footprints of past bears and their paw marks make a line of holes in the ground.

We walked until my feet were sore and aching. But I don't want to complain. I'm really excited to be out in the wild, even if I'm a bit scared about what we might find.

Jack says there are mountains around us. But the rain and low clouds block the view like a soggy blanket. So far, we haven't seen a trace of the bears, but Jack's sure they're out there. Somewhere ahead. Somewhere…

BATTLE OF THE BEARS

September 3

We were up at five this morning without a steaming cup of tea to start the day. Jack said we couldn't light a fire because the flames and smoke might frighten away Honey and the cubs.

Today I scoffed Grainy Crunch and munched the meat with relish. Then I asked Jack for seconds. That's what hunger does to you.

Like yesterday, we spent the day walking. I'm not allowed to tell you where we are, but to be honest, I'm not sure myself! I think we're close to the Paint River. Jack says some bear hunters could read the exact details in this diary and go looking for Honey. They would think nothing of shooting her for her lovely fur coat.

This afternoon I had a worrying thought. What if we're heading in the wrong direction?

"So how come you're so sure Honey went this way?" I asked Jack as we plodded along.

He smiled. "Last autumn I tracked Honey and the cubs this way. I was trying to find out where they went for the winter. I lost them, but I figure Honey has a den somewhere around here. She's probably heading back there now."

BEN'S BEAR NOTES

DENS

1. **The den is usually a short tunnel leading to a hole dug out of the earth. There's just enough room for a sleeping bear's bedroom.**
2. **The den is often on a north-facing slope where the snow builds up. Up to 60 cm of snow can cover the den, and it actually helps to keep the cold out.**

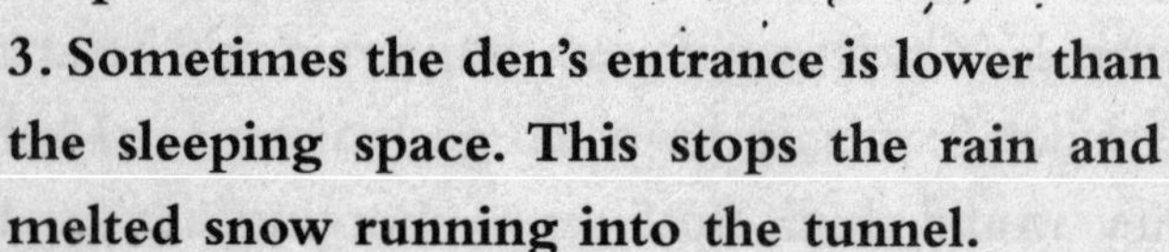

3. **Sometimes the den's entrance is lower than the sleeping space. This stops the rain and melted snow running into the tunnel.**

September 4

Still no bears, but this morning we found a tuft of honey-coloured fur in a thorny bush. Further on we came across a slimy salmon covered in squirming maggots. The stink made me gasp for air and wave my hand in front of my mouth. Most of the fish had been eaten. By a bear, Jack says. Maybe it was Honey?

Jack's strict about where we can camp. We can't be too close to bushes or water because that's where bears often take naps. It would be a very bad idea to fall out with the local bears. Maybe that's why we always end up camping in the most rocky, boggy, windy places in Alaska. Last night it rained and I slept in a puddle.

I'm hungry. "FOOD, FOOD, FOOD, FOOD, FOOD!" growls my stomach. I'm not interested in a tub of chocolate-chip ice cream any more, I want a bucket of it! All to myself. But I'm not fussy – I'll never, ever, moan about spicy noodle surprise again, I promise! I want to get out of the rain and I want to be warm. I want to go back to camp and drink hot coffee in the sauna. But I can't – not until I know the cubs are safe.

September 5

We walked and walked and walked. Then we walked some more.

Despite what I said yesterday about not wanting to go back to the camp, I was just about ready to tell Jack I'd had enough. Then I spotted a distant splash of pale fur. With a dry mouth and pounding heart I fumbled with my binoculars. I held the binoculars to my eyes and sure enough, it was Honey! Was she alone? No – the cubs were with her! So Rocky was OK!

But then Jack gave a low whistle and grabbed my sleeve. "Look over there!" he hissed.

I followed his pointing finger. I could see a dark shape in a patch of bushes. It was something big. Something alive. With a nasty shock, I recognized the dark shape as a bear. It was Slasher!

"What's he doing here?" I asked anxiously. Jack shook his head. "I can't say. Maybe Slasher's got a den around here."

"But what's he up to now?" I demanded.

"We'd best go and take a look," said Jack. " But we

don't want the bears to see us – they could run or attack us. We'll get a better chance if we split up. You circle to the left and I'll go right. Try to keep to the bushes. Don't get too close. If a bear comes your way, back off."

I nodded. I hoped I looked calm to Jack, but inside my blood was zipping through my veins. I felt my heart – it seemed about to go POP!

Quite soon I saw that I had the more tricky task. The path I was following amongst bushes and wet grass was nothing more than a line of bare earth. I crouched low so the bears couldn't see me. But now I couldn't see the bears either. I imagined Slasher creeping up on me.

I heard rushing water. Ahead, the ground sloped down to a small valley with a waterfall at the bottom. It wasn't as big as McNeil Falls, but it was loud and busy. I would have to cross the stream with care. I was just about to head off down the slope when I heard growling. There were two bears fighting on the other side of the valley. It was Honey and Slasher!

Honey and Slasher were too busy biting each other to notice me. I hid behind a bush and watched breathlessly through my binoculars. Slasher's larger weight forced Honey down the slope. She dropped down on all fours and the cubs followed her. I heard the cubs above the noise of the waterfall – they were screaming with fear. They were trying to hide behind their mum. But Honey was bleeding.

Slasher charged again. This time he chased Honey up the slope and away from her cubs. Away from their mum, Rocky and Sandy had no defence. If Slasher had turned on them, they were as good as dead.

I knew what I had to do and I knew it was dangerous. With wobbly legs and a thumping heart, I stepped out from behind the bush. Jack said we shouldn't get involved but I knew I had to. All I was thinking was, "I've got to save Rocky and Sandy!"

From across the stream, Slasher saw me. He stared at me. It was a bear's version of a dirty look. "Back off or it'll be worse for you!" he seemed to snarl.

I shook my head. I felt as if the big bear was actually talking to me.

Then I remembered how Brett had talked to bears. I knew Slasher couldn't understand, but that didn't stop me.

"Hello, Slasher," I said. My voice sounded much too high. "My name is Ben Adams. I'm a teacher. I've been writing a diary about that cub – Rocky – the one you're about to kill."

Slasher grunted and stood up on his hind legs. He looked gigantic and I could see the rippling muscles under his sleek dark fur. But I carried on talking.

"I can't let you do it," I gasped. "I came to Alaska to see bears. But now I'm bonded. I'm bonded to that cub. And it would break my heart if he died!"

Slasher opened his mouth and showed me his big, yellow, slobber-dripping fangs. His small mean eyes blazed red and angry.

"Back off!" I squeaked. "I'm not scared of you – you big bear bully!"

Slasher dropped down onto all fours. His jaws moved as he ground his teeth in rage. Then he charged. He was coming straight at me!

My brain wanted to run. But my feet seemed to have grown roots. So I just stood still.

"And I'm not afraid!" I wailed in terror.

Amazingly, Slasher stopped at the stream. Big splats of mud flew through the air as he skidded to a halt on the slippery wet grass. Then the big bear lowered his head and took a deep angry gulp of water. With a final menacing look, he stalked off up the valley. Slasher had been trying a mock charge. If I'd tried to run, I'd have been dead.

All this time my whole world had narrowed down to the big dark bear. But now I noticed the cubs creeping towards Honey, who was watching from the top of the slope. I began to laugh nervously. "I've done it! I've done it! Rocky is safe!" I cried.

I was laughing so much, I lost my footing. I slipped and hit the ground. I rolled down the slope. The world whizzed around me. I had grass in my mouth and earth in my ears. "This is silly," I thought. "Why can't I stop?" And then I did stop. I hit the water. All I could see was wet white foam. And all I could hear was water – rushing, rushing, rushing.

It felt like ages but it can only have been seconds. I sat up in the water. I felt cold and wet and shivering and sore. And my left arm felt oddly stiff.

Then I saw Rocky at the top of the slope. I could see seagulls flying over his head like blossom blown off a tree. Rocky was just staring up at them. I staggered to my feet and climbed out of the stream. I was trying to be really careful. I didn't want to fall in again!

I must have been dazed because it took me ages to notice that the bears had gone. I didn't see them go. But Jack was running towards me.

"Are you all right?" he called.

I nodded, but I knew I wasn't.

September 6

Jack reckons I've broken my arm. My arm feels too stiff to move and I didn't get much sleep last night.

It's been misty all day. We don't have a radio and in this mist no rescue plane will be able to find us. So I know we have to walk back to the camp.

Every step hurts my arm. It's hard to walk with my arm in a sling. Jack's made the sling from his dirty old vest. It's a bit smelly, but I'm past caring.

September 7

Now I'm injured, Jack lights a fire at night. This evening as we sat watching the flames, Jack told me the sad tale of bears and people.

Once upon a time, there were no people in America. The whole vast land belonged to its animals. And the smartest of all these creatures were the bears. Brown bears walked across the strip of land that joined Asia to Alaska 50,000 years ago. They spread out and, in time, found their way south to Mexico.

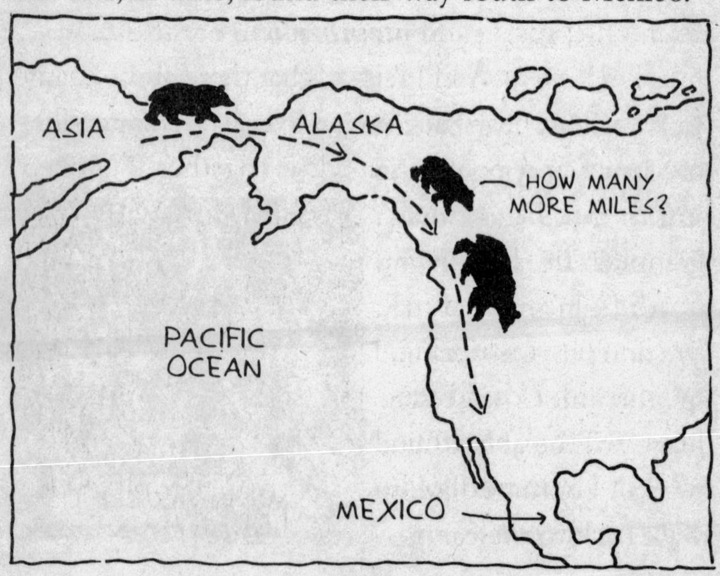

"Everything changed," said Jack, "when people showed up. Humans had bows and arrows. They knew how to kill bears. But things were still just about OK. The native people of America believed bears had wise spirits. So they didn't hunt them too often."

"What went wrong?" I asked, trying to forget my aching arm. I was thinking about Teddy Roosevelt and his bear hunt.

Jack sighed. "Guns," he said in a disgusted voice. "Settlers from Europe with their guns and cows and sheep. Bears hate sheep. It's something about them dumb, bleating animals that makes bears mad. The bears killed them. So the farmers shot the bears. In state after state they drove out or killed all the bears. There used to be about 100,000 and today there's around half that – and most of them are in Alaska."

Jack fell silent. And I felt sad that there are so many places where bears no longer live. It seems terrible that bears and people can't live together. I looked at Jack but he seemed wrapped in his own thoughts. His eyes were dark and he was tugging at his beard. I could see there was something else on his mind. So I asked him about it.

Jack sighed heavily. "Ben, have you ever done anything for which you are really, truly sorry?" he asked.

I thought hard. All I could think of was squeezing my little brother's finger in the door when he was three and I was six.

Jack shook his head. "Heck no – that's kids' stuff, I mean something *real* bad. Something that sticks with you for years, that gets to you at night sometimes so you wake up in a cold sweat."

I shrugged my shoulders and winced as a stab of pain shot up my arm.

Jack forced a tight little smile. "Well I guess you're a lucky guy. I've got something on my mind and it's been gnawing away since I was 16. You're the first living soul I've ever told." There was a short silence as Jack collected his thoughts.

"It was about this time of year. I was trekking in the mountains with my dog, Scratch. We'd come across an old cabin and I was fixing supper when I heard barking. I looked out the door and there was Scratch snarling and snapping at something. And what d'you think he'd found? It was a grizzly bear cub. It couldn't have been more than eight months old. Well, I tried to pull the dog off the bear. But no sooner had I grabbed Scratch when the bear leaped at him, biting and clawing. The cub was badly hurt but it was still hanging in there. That little fella had the heart of a lion!"

"What happened to it?" I asked. I had a nasty feeling that I already knew.

Jack shook his head and sighed. "The little fella didn't make it. He was too badly hurt." Jack sighed again and this time there were tears in his eyes.

"I've always felt bad about that cub, like it was my fault. If I hadn't been making cooking smells, the bear wouldn't have sniffed out the cabin. If I'd tied the dog up, the bear wouldn't have been hurt. I've never taken a dog out in the wild since." He stopped suddenly and looked at me. "I s'pose you think I'm being stupid?" he demanded.

"No," I said. "But now I know why you were so keen on finding our bears."

Jack nodded slowly. "Hmm – I can see what you're getting at. It kinda adds up."

September 9

This afternoon the weather began to brighten as the mist lifted. For the first time this week I saw the mountains and little splashes of blue sky amongst the clouds. In the far distance I could see a strip of shiny silvery water in the afternoon light. It was McNeil Cove. I knew we'd be home tonight.

September 12

OK, so I'll come clean. The last few days diary weren't written on the days I said they were. I wrote them all just now. I mean, how could I write when I was in such pain?

My arm is broken. The doctors here at the hospital in Homer X-rayed my arm and I've seen the pictures. My arm's in a plaster cast now and I'm resting in bed. Ever since Jack and I arrived back at the camp, I've had to answer questions, questions, and more questions.

We flew to Homer yesterday. The red-and-white plane was parked in the water by the beach. Jack helped me into the plane and Molly and Brett carried my rucksack. You won't believe how much you need your arms when you climb into a small plane.

"Let's get this baby into the air!" said Hank as he finished his pre-flight checks. Then the small plane bumped into the air and we waved goodbye to McNeil River.

Well, that was yesterday. And today, I've had the whole day to wonder how my bears are getting on.

Right now, I guess, they'll be snuggled up for the night. I imagine them cuddled together for warmth on a cosy bed of moss and leaves. The bears will feast on berries until the first winter snowflakes drift down on their thick fur. Then Honey will take them to their winter den for their long sleep.

For me, it's time to leave Alaska. Tomorrow Jack's driving me back to Anchorage, and the day after tomorrow I'll be catching a flight home. Like the bears, I'm ready for a good long sleep!

ROCKY – WHERE ARE YOU?

July 6 – ten months later

I've been back at school and teaching since November. I even did a talk on my adventures for children and parents. Everyone clapped at the end, although they did laugh when Mr Henley reminded them about the day I'd dressed up as a bear.

But even when I'm at school I can't stop wondering what happened to the bears. Although Wildwatch are going to turn my diary into a book, I don't want to finish it until I'm sure that Rocky and Sandy are still alive. And right now I can't be too certain…

What if the cold weather froze the cubs in their den? This can happen in really bitter winters. What if the bears couldn't find enough food when they woke up and starved to death?

The only way I can find out if the bears are OK is if they show up at McNeil River this summer. If the bears are alive they'll be arriving any day now. Jack's back at the camp, working as a ranger, and he's written me a letter. He says that Molly and Brett are fine, but there's been no sign of Honey and her cubs.

This year there's a web-cam camera at the Falls. You can actually watch the bears on the Internet. So every day I log on and watch and hope that I'll see Rocky. Of course, I haven't seen him yet. Today my computer broke down, but I've got a back-up plan. Tomorrow I'm going to stay behind after school and use the computer in the library.

July 7

This evening I sat in the library watching the bears. On the web-cam they appeared to move jerkily, just like an old movie. It was hard to believe I was seeing real bears mooching around at that very second thousands of kilometres away.

Anyway, I was just thinking how amazing the technology was when I noticed a young, clumsy-looking bear.

"Hey – that bear looks just like Scruffy!" I said to myself. I peered more closely at the computer screen. And guess what? The bear really *was* Scruffy!

Just then an annoying fly buzzed in my ear. I smacked my ear and missed the fly.

I looked back at the screen just in time to see a straw-coloured bear ambling into view. She was a female, and she had two cheerful cubs jogging along behind her. Could it be? YES – it *was* Honey, and the cubs were Rocky and Sandy! THEY LOOKED GREAT!

I noticed with excitement that Rocky was bigger than Sandy. He looked big enough to jump on top of me and knock me flying!

I cheered out loud. "Yes!" I yelled. "YES – the cubs are back!"

Mrs Dwyer gave me a disapproving look. "Now then, Mr Adams," she said. "Just because there are no children here, there's no excuse for that kind of behaviour!"

"But it's the best day of my life!" I cried. "I'm so happy I could sing!" And with that I began to sing, "Today's the day the teddy bears have their pic-nic!"

I watched the bears until Mrs Dwyer was standing at the library door, jangling her keys. As I left I felt as if I was walking on air, and I drove home full of warm, happy feelings.

Later

Now I can finish my story. And tomorrow I'll put this diary in the post to Wildwatch.

I look up at the dark blue sky. Tonight the stars are bright and twinkling. High in the sky, there's a group of stars called the Little Bear. In ancient times, people thought it looked like a bear cub. But I can't see it myself.

Below the Little Bear is another set of stars called the Big Dipper. It's also called the Great Bear. If you watch the sky all night you'll see the Great Bear and the Little Bear chasing each other around. All night long, as the Earth spins in space, the bears dance in a great circle in the night sky.

And that gets me thinking about real bears. The beautiful brown bears fishing and feasting by their lovely river of silver fish. And most of all I think about a special, brave, naughty little cub named Rocky. I just can't help it – you see I'm still bonded to that bear.